James Rice, Walter Besant

With Harp and Crown

Vol. II

James Rice, Walter Besant

With Harp and Crown
Vol. II

ISBN/EAN: 9783337067854

Printed in Europe, USA, Canada, Australia, Japan

Cover: Foto ©Andreas Hilbeck / pixelio.de

More available books at **www.hansebooks.com**

WITH HARP AND CROWN.

A Novel.

BY THE AUTHORS OF

"READY-MONEY MORTIBOY,"

"MY LITTLE GIRL," "THIS SON OF VULCAN," ETC.

IN THREE VOLUMES.

.VOL. II.

LONDON:

TINSLEY BROTHERS, 8, CATHERINE STREET,

STRAND.

———

1875.

LONDON:
SWEETING AND CO., PRINTERS,
80, GRAY'S INN ROAD.

WITH HARP AND CROWN.

CHAPTER I.

MR. RHYL OWEN sat opposite, watching his guest with loving eyes. He was a soft-hearted creature, though he was the master of a Commercial Academy; and it went to his heart to think that this fair young creature should actually want the commonest necessaries of life. He cut the bread and poured out the tea with zealous solicitude.

"Is it good? is it refreshing?" asked he. "Now, do have another slice—some more bread: eat plenty of bread with it; and now the tea—we must do without the milk, because I've drunk it all up myself—a greedy beast! Some people like a bloater with a meat tea. I say bacon's more wholesome. As for sprats, now, I suppose a young lady like you wouldn't look at them."

"I would have looked at anything five minutes ago. Oh, Mr. Owen, I am so much obliged. It is so horrid to be hungry."

She finished her tea, and then looked up, with her familiar laugh.

"That's right," he nodded, and smiled back. "Already you look filled out in the cheeks, in a manner of speaking; though you're not, no more than your sister, like my Winifred for plumpness. Tell me, Miss Adie, you are not often so bad as this upstairs, eh?"

"I don't think we have ever been quite so bad before, even before Marion was able to sell her sketches. But then we have been thrown back. It was necessary for Fred, who must have a good appearance when he goes into the City to look for a secretaryship, to have a new suit of clothes, with a great-coat, this weather. That took all our spare money, as you may guess. Then we have had to pawn things—my father's watch and chain, and even his sword. You may think how Marion liked that."

"My dear, you had better not tell me more

than you think right," said Mr. Owen, with some delicacy about hearing further particulars.

"Why not? It is no use pretending to be proud—we have nothing to conceal; we have been ladies and gentlemen—now we are not, I suppose. What else is there to say? There is no shame in being poor."

She laughed, but she spoke a little bitterly.

"Poor Miss Marion!"

"Yes, it's hardest on Marion, isn't it? because she does all the work for us. Besides, she was the eldest, and had been most with poor papa. I hope she will bring some money home with her."

"Perhaps your brother—"

"Oh," she laughed again, "Fred never brings any money home; he takes all the money out. But that will do about myself. How have the boys been to-day—good?"

"Boys never are good. They are born bad—original sin, you know—and it is our duty to thrash them till they grow good. Listen, there's some one at the door again. If it is Mrs. Candy, she is coming to have a row. Perhaps it's— Why"—his face lit up all over with pleasure —"it's actually Winifred, home two hours before I expected her."

It was Winifred. She came running into the room, threw her arms about her father, and gave him two great smacks, one on each cheek; then caught Adie by the chin, held her face up to the light critically, and kissed that too.

"You are the prettiest girl in all London," she whispered.

Then she took the lid off the tea pot and examined its contents, put in some water, and got another cup and saucer. Then she threw off her hat and jacket; and then, everything ready, she sat down and prepared to enjoy herself in a businesslike manner.

"It is perfectly delicious," she said. "Tea made, Adie to tea with us, and a fire. Father, this is worth living for, isn't it?"

He sucked his pipe and nodded.

"Bread and butter, Adie, dear. How sorry I am I wasn't home to have tea with you! No, I won't have any bacon, thank you. There are times, father, when you feel yourself a man to be envied, eh? Your daughter in the Civil Service, like a proud young competitive clerk; a young lady to tea with you; and your work for the day done. Good work, too. Adie, I am always proud of my father's work."

She read her father's moods by his face, and spoke accordingly.

"I tell him," Winifred continued, looking sideways at the little cloud which still hung upon her father's brow—"I tell him it is noble work which he is doing, the best work a man can do, to raise these poor boys out of ignorance, to bear with their ways, and try to make them like himself."

Mr. Owen shook his head with mild deprecation. But he enjoyed it.

"Nonsense, father! Every teacher wants to make his disciples like himself, else what would be the good of teaching? A schoolmaster ought to be learned; you are learned, father."

"Pretty well, my dear, pretty well. Cæsar at my fingers' ends, as you may say; and as far as Compound Interest, perhaps, you might find it hard to meet my match."

"He must be sober. Why, father, who could be soberer than you?"

"Yes, my dear; I am too poor to drink if I wanted to."

"He must be just."

Mr. Owen nodded, as much as to say that Lowland-street Academy contained the justest of men.

"Merciful, too, with his justice."

He nodded again, with emphasis.

"By the way, father, who was that I heard crying yesterday?"

"Candy Secundus," said her father, shortly.

"Poor Candy Secundus! Poor little Sugar Candy! Do you know little Sugar Candy, Adie? The dearest little fellow, with blue eyes and curly hair, and always getting into scrapes. His mother keeps the baker's shop over the way. What did poor Sugar Candy do, father?"

"Justice comes before mercy," said Rhyl Owen. "'Chastise thy son while there is hope, and let not thy soul spare for his crying.' Candy Secundus brought a piece of chalk in his trousers pocket, and chalked upon my desk —my desk—these lines:—

'Taffy is a Welshman;
Taffy keeps a cane;
When I get a big man
He shall have it back again.'

Candy Secundus will remember his verses for some time when he comes to sit down. I expect Candy's mother will come to-night to give notice."

Winifred looked graver. The withdrawal of one boy from the little school meant the loss of a pound a quarter, a sensible item in the modest household.

"I will go round and see her presently," she said. "Perhaps she will be reasonable."

As the light fell upon her, the low fire on the left and the gas just turned on overhead made pretty effects of colour in the twilight. You may see that she is not a beautiful girl—not beautiful in the sense that Adie, with her regular features and calm eyes in a perpetual repose, is beautiful. Look again: you see a face full of mirth and animation; a nose rather short and perhaps a little too broad; lips half open, showing the whitest teeth behind; and more still, cheeks as soft as peaches and set with a pair of dimples— *petites fossettes d'amour.* Her chin is strongly accentuated and rather pointed, for Winifred has a will of her own; the tiniest and daintiest little pink ears nestle beneath a cloud of rebel-

lious locks of light brown, which escape from
their assigned places, and float at their own
sweet will; a face full of affection, enjoyment,
and possible passion; and, to crown all, a pair
of grey eyes which have caught the sunshine of
June, and give it back through all the year—eyes
always ready to laugh; eyes fearless and trust-
ing; eyes that enjoy the world, and are aglow
with the fire of her youthful blood, in which the
lover—when the lover comes—will see "a foun-
tain of gardens, a well of living waters, and
streams from Lebanon." Her fingers, long and
delicate, quiver when she speaks, as if she was
working the telegraph still. As she sits, as
she moves, as she speaks, you feel that you
are with a girl whose nervous system is
strung by nature to concert pitch, so that one
note out of tune would set the whole ajar. The
other girl, Adie Revel, beside her, is at present
calmly and dispassionately happy. She has had
enough to eat—that is sufficient for the time.
Like the owner of the Splendid Shilling, she can
say, "Fate cannot harm me; I have dined to-
day." She has no more care for the next day
than when we left her last, playing Badminton

with her brother. Like the soft-eyed deer, she lies in the sun and warmth, enjoys what the present has to give, and is a philosopher in this—that she leaves the gods the rest. "Heaven," we know, "which sees the future, keeps the issues in the darkness of the night; nor does it forgive the man who trembles before what is coming, more than is due to human uncertainty." Adie had never read Horace; but she agreed with so much of his philosophy as not to tremble at thinking of the future. Now Winifred thought perpetually of things that might be coming: she thought of Marion, who worked for the three; of Adie, who could not work, but sat at home and hoped for better things; and she thought—she thought too much—of Fred: Fred the handsome, Fred the indolent, Fred, whose very faults made him interesting, because they were not the faults of the class among whom she had been brought up. A young man of Lowland-street or Euphrates-row, if he departed from the paths of rectitude, which was not uncommon, was to be seen smoking pipes at public-house doors, reeling home at night, or even, in extreme cases of moral obliquity, marching handcuffed between

two men in blue, or escorted from the doors of
Bow-street Police-office to the door of her Majesty's omnibus. The Lowland-street youth did
not, like Mr. Frederick Revel, wear trousers and
coat closely resembling those of Bond-street; they
did not spend the day in the fashionable end of
the town; they did not frequent West-end billiard
rooms; nor did they despise the companionship
of other young gentlemen in the street. Perhaps
it was the contrast of Fred Revel with this
other young man which made Winifred think
so much about him.

The old schoolmaster, retreating from the
table to his place in the window and his book,
left the two girls to their talk.

"Poor dear!" said Winifred. "To think of
your going without your dinner for two days!
Why did you not tell us?"

Adie laughed.

"That is nothing, providing we don't have to
go without our dinner to-morrow and the next
day. But I dare say Marion will get some
money; she always does find money somehow."

"Perhaps your brother will get a proper place
soon."

"Poor Fred! He says, Winifred, that some people are born to work and some to spend, and he certainly was not born to work. Sometimes I think that Fred never will get any more work to do at all. You know, he does try; he goes into the City, I believe, at least once a week—and everybody knows it is in the City that you pick up rich posts. Once he was made secretary to a company. His friend, Lord Rodney Benbow, got him the post. To be sure, the company broke up in a month; but then, as Fred says, it gave him the business experience that he wanted. Winifred, don't let Marion know that I told you about our distress; she is proud, and would not like it. As if it matters now," she said, with a bitter laugh—"as if it matters for all the world to know how poor we are! Let them know. We have not had a single friend to care whether we starve or not."

"Oh, Adie, you have me."

"It is a horrid thing to be poor," she went on, passionately. "It is a cruel thing, a wrong thing, a wretched thing to be poor. Marion seems to think it enough if we get our miserable meals day by day."

"Give us this day our daily bread, Adie," said Winifred.

"I know. But my bread ought to be more than breakfast and dinner and tea. I want things, Winifred, that other girls have. What is the good of life where there is no pleasure— nothing but working day after day to get enough to eat?"

"But we cannot have all we want to have," said the telegraph girl, letting her thoughts loose vaguely in the field of boundless impossibilities.

"Why can't we? Once I had all that I wanted; it was not much, to be sure, for I was only sixteen, and satisfied with little. Now I am twenty, I want to live."

"Adie, do you think it is right to talk so."

"Right or not, I do so because I think so. Yesterday I went out with Fred for a walk. He will not take me to Regent-street or the Park, for fear of meeting his old college friends. You see, Winifred, this is the only dress I have got. I can trim it up after the fashion, but I can't turn it into a new dress. Fred keeps up appearances better—I do not know how. Well, he is ashamed to be seen with his sisters in the street.

We walked part of the way down Oxford-street, turned to the right up Berners-street, and then, after seven o'clock, when all the gentlemen were having dinner, and Fred was not afraid of meeting any one he knew, we went down Bond-street and Piccadilly. As we came home through the squares, the people were driving off to dinner; in one or two houses we could see them sitting down, ladies and gentlemen—ah, happy people! —dining properly, and with servants to wait. Some other people, not so happy, but better off than ourselves, were going to the theatres. We came home. Neither Fred nor I had a single sixpence between us. When we got home, we found Marion sitting with a single light, trying to draw an outline. She had no money either. Fred smoked, nobody spoke, because we were all three too miserable; and about ten we went to bed. We had had neither tea nor supper, and Marion sat all the evening with her head on her hand. Poor Marion! Poor Fred! Poor me! You don't mean, Winifred, that I should like this life ?"

A grunt escaped the lips of the schoolmaster, but he said nothing. Adie looked up a moment, and went on, in a lower voice—

"Fred keeps up his spirits and mine too, as well as he can, the dear fellow. He is always cheerful; he says that something will happen to make us all comfortable again. But it is worse for Marion, because she has all the work to do, poor thing! She is different from both of us, I think; and takes things more seriously. To be sure, where should we be without her?"

"When Fred — I mean your brother," said Winifred—"gets the place he wants, it will be better, will it not? He will do something for you. It would be dreadful for him to go on for ever allowing Marion to work for both of you."

"That is what he says and thinks. Fred has, only you would not think it unless you knew him as well I do, the noblest of hearts. He says that this living on the proceeds of Marion's work is killing him, and I am sure that he is getting thinner. He declares that he is ready to take any kind of work that offers. Of course, you know, Winifred, it must be such work as a gentleman can do. Now and then Dr. Chacomb suggests something; but Fred has got an aver-sion to the doctor, and his way of looking at things. Above all, as Fred says, he is a gentle-man, and, if he pleased, a nobleman."

"Yes, dear, I know."

There was another grunt from the school-master.

" I read once," he said, without looking round, " of a nobleman in France who fell into poverty. He resolved on giving up his title and forgetting his rank. He handed his sword to the Mayor of Bordeaux, and went away. When he came home after twenty years, enriched by trade, he demanded back, and received again, the sword of his ancestors."

Adie listened politely.

"You had better tell Fred that story, Mr. Owen," she said, with a laugh. "I should like to see Fred depositing my father's sword with the Lord Mayor of London while he went about, on Dr. Chacomb's suggestion, as an ad-vertising tout. That was the last advice, I be-lieve."

"There are good families in Wales," said Rhyl Owen, "as well as in France. My father, Ap Rhyl, whose father was Ap Owen, used to boast of our descent from Llewellyn, who was a king.

living, and never grumbled at it."

"Never mind, father," said Winifred. "You do not quite understand."

But Adie, disinclined to discuss the question, had risen.

"I shall go upstairs now," she said. "Good night, Mr. Owen." She went to the chair, and held out her hands. "I am very, very much obliged to you."

"Child," said the schoolmaster, looking up at her, "stoop down, and let me whisper. If you have got no money to-morrow, you and your sister come down here at one o'clock—we will go shares. And, Miss Adie, make your brother do some work, and try to get some for yourself. Don't leave everything to Miss Marion."

Adie nodded her head, laughed, kissed him on the forehead, and left him. It was two years since they came to the house. Rhyl Owen and his daughter were not, as she and Fred confessed to each other, strictly of the upper classes, but they were kind. Adie loved little attentions, and craved for the outside signs of affec tion. Winifred was her only companion, and,

when Fred was not at home, she allowed herself
a greater approach to familiarity with Winifred's
father than her aristocratic brother would have
approved of. At all events, she felt that he
would have shuddered if he had seen her actually kiss the forehead of the little Welsh schoolmaster.

"Not even a University man!" he would have
said.

"Winifred," said her father, abruptly, "he's
a worthless chap."

Winifred changed colour. But she knew
whom he meant.

"He's a worthless chap, Winifred, my girl,"
he went on. "He hangs about billiard tables,
and borrows money of gentlemen. Sam Beagle,
who is head waiter at the Guards' Club, told me
he heard Lord Rodney talking about him, saying that Fred Revel cost him a sovereign every
time he met him, and he'd be dashed if he'd
stand it any longer."

Winifred was silent still.

"As for the girls—the young ladies, I mean
—it's a good thing for you and me that they
came here. It isn't often that we get the chance

of knowing a real lady. As for Miss Marion—
Lord! when I think of that girl, Winifred, and
how she toils and slaves, my blood boils—it
boils, I say. There, I've broken my pipe!
Give me the other one, my dear. As for Miss
Marion, I say, she's a good woman. Who can
say more?"

He got up, and stood before the spark that
lingered in the fireplace.

"What does Solomon say about a good
woman?" He took a Bible, and opened it at
the Book of Proverbs, and read—"'She riseth
while it is yet night, and giveth meat to the
household. . . Strength and honour are her
clothing ; and she shall rejoice in time to come.
. . . In her tongue is the law of kindness. . . .
Many daughters have done virtuously, but she
excels them all. . . Let her own works praise
her in the gates.' That is Marion Revel. I
have watched her for two years. She is the
good woman of Solomon, and she is more—
she is the true Christian, Winifred, because she
thinks and works for others, and not for herself."

"And so do you, father, dear."

He stroked his chin.

"In a measure, my child. Yes. It is the task of the teacher, I read in a book the other day, to lose his own interests in those of his pupil. The anxieties of one become the sufferings of the other; he feels with his scholar—"

"Poor little Sugar Candy," said Winifred, thoughtfully, with a gleam in her eye.

Her father caught it, and laughed. He was a silent man out of school, because he talked so much in school hours that quiet was needful. He was a grave man, because he could not indulge in the natural mirth of his nature before the boys; but the old Adam broke out sometimes, as it did now.

"Ho! ho!" he laughed. "Candy Secundus will become a great poet:

> 'Taffy was a Welshman;
>   Taffy had a big cane;
> When I get a big man
>   He shall have it back again.'

Ho! ho! ho! If little Candy does turn out a great man, my dear, they will tell of this day, and how his brutal schoolmaster flogged him. Dear me! Schoolmasters are a misrepresented

race! I dare say Orbilius in Francis's 'Horace'
—there is the book on the top shelf—was a
merry, soft-hearted, and gentle creature, only
Horace never understood the right side of his
nature. Perhaps Busby used to cry at night
when he thought of all the boys wriggling on
their seats."

"Winifred," he went on again, after a few
meditative puffs of his pipe, "think over what I
said, my dear. He is a worthless chap. You
went for a walk with him on Sunday afternoon."

"Yes, father, but Adie was with us. Oh, you
don't know!" She took his face in her hands,
and squeezed the wrinkled and crow's-footed
eyes and nose together. "You don't know anything about it, father. Why, the Revels are
quite above us. Fred is a gentleman, an Oxford
man, a scholar, and a Count—think of that—
only he is too proud to take the title. And
what am I? Only a telegraph girl, father."

She laughed as she spoke, but the tears came
into her eyes. She brushed them away quickly.

"And now, father, I shall go round to Mrs.
Candy's, and find out if she is angry with you.

I shall pretend to ask for a loaf, you know. We can't have the school dropping to pieces just yet, can we? Dear old father, you have yet to work a year or two longer, until your daughter can make money enough to keep you."

Left alone, the schoolmaster sat down and pondered. The house was quiet and lonely. He thought of his bright and pretty girl; he thought of the idler whose fancy she had caught; he wondered what was best to be done. Outside the house, in the street, the children shouted and played; within there was the silence of the grave. And he thought of the two friendless girls above him, and one of them so helpless.

"Between most of us and starvation," he said, "there's only the mercy of the Lord. Thank Him, it's a thickish plank."

Presently he heard a heavy foot mount the stairs, and stop at the Revels' door.

CHAPTER II.

THE visitor knocked at Miss Revel's door. Getting no reply, he gently turned the handle and looked in. Its only occupant, Adie, was sitting in the dusk at one of the windows, pressing her cheek against the glass, and gazing, with her thoughts far away, at the passers below. The gas from the street and the shop over the way lit up the room. In the softened twilight and the dim illumination you could perceive that the room was comfortably furnished with easy chairs, a sofa, a piano, and a few water-colour paintings. The light was not strong enough to show that the covering of chairs and sofa was worn in holes and faded, that the carpet was ragged, that the piano bore marks of age and use. An easel stood at one window, and by it a small stand with paints and canvas. In the centre was a table covered with work, over which Adie's fingers had been busy during the day. She was not idle, for she kept the wardrobe of her sister and herself, and maintained, in spite of all difficulties, the neatness of her brother's linen. The new-comer, who was indeed no other than Dr. Chacomb, stepped across with the noiseless tread affected by some heavy men, and laid his hand gently on Adie's.

"You?" she started. "I did not hear any one open the door. I thought you had deserted us, Dr. Chacomb. It is nearly six months since you came to see us last."

"I got very little encouragement in my last visit," he said. "I am not quite certain that I ought to come here again at all."

"Did Fred say anything to annoy you? You remember that you annoyed *him* very much."

"So that he had the right to annoy me in return, you mean. No, it was not your brother's little outbreak of temper. I hardly know what that young man could do which would annoy me. He might surprise me, certainly. If he were to get his living in any honest way, it would surprise me. But he would never annoy me."

"Do not say unkind things about Fred," said Adie. "For my own part, I should be extremely sorry to have him making his living as an advertising tout; and that, you know, was what you advised him to become."

"That is about the only thing he is fit for," said the doctor.

"Well, if it was not Fred, who was it—Marion or myself?"

"As it was not you, it was of course your sister."

"I declare," said Adie, pettishly, "it is too provoking. What did Marion say or do, I should like to know? You are absolutely the only decent creature left in the world—not to speak of dear little Winifred Owen—that comes to see us, and you take offence at some nonsensical fancy of your own. Oh, why are men so stupid?"

"Hardly a nonsensical fancy," said the doctor. "It was real hard fact. Where is Marion?"

"I do not know. She went to Burls's shop. Perhaps she stayed there to finish off something;

perhaps she had to go over Waterloo Bridge to Hermann's. She may be in any moment. Sit down and be comfortable, and tell me all about it."

"Tell me first how you have been getting on since last I saw you."

"We have been getting on worse and worse. I think we did have some money, a little, left when you came last. That is all gone now. And Marion has not been doing very well for the last three months. At present, we have nothing."

"Nothing?"

"Nothing at all. Not a sixpence in the world. We paid our rent for the quarter out of Marion's dividends. Then we had a little money left to live upon; we have got nothing now, and out of that we have to save up for next quarter's rent, and live besides. It's like what papa used to call a midshipman's half-pay."

The doctor was silent.

"Yesterday we had no dinner. To-day we have had no dinner. I do not know what poor Marion has done; but I went downstairs, when I was so hungry that I could not bear myself any

longer, and asked Mr. Owen to give me something to eat. I've had bacon, and bread and
butter and tea."

"And Fred?"

"Fred is like the sparrows: he picks up his
dinner in the street," said Adie. "I wish I
could."

"No money, no dinner. Why did you not
send to me, child?"

"Why did you not come to us?"

"Did not Marion tell you anything?"

"No. Marion tells me nothing about herself.
Tell me what was the matter, Dr. Chacomb.
Perhaps I can help to put things right. Heaven knows we can't afford to give up our only
friend."

"It is a very simple matter," he replied. "I
asked Marion to marry me, and she refused."

"Oh!"

Adie found nothing else to say before a statement the whole bearing of which she could not
immediately realize.

"You, too, I suppose, think it absurd," said
Dr. Chacomb.

"I have never thought anything about it at

all," she replied; "because this is the only time I have heard about it. But it does seem at first as if it was too bad that you can't know us without wanting to marry one of us. Why isn't all the stupid love taken out of the novels? No one would think of it at all unless for them—I am sure Marion and I don't—and then we could live together and be happy."

"Childish talk," said the doctor. "You don't understand. Now listen, Adie, and see if you can understand this. When you knew me four years ago, I had no money, and was in debt. I used to run down to Chacomb to borrow, when I was hard up, of poor Chauncey. I had a mouldy little surgery—I blush to think of it— at Islington, with half a dozen patients, and what is called a general practice. I was lazy, because I had nothing to do. I was forty-five years of age, and a failure. You remember me then. Try to compare me now with what I was. Tell me what you thought of me."

Adie laughed, and shut her eyes. It was great fun to tell Dr. Chacomb the exact truth, and not to offend him.

"I shall not be complimentary," she said.

"You were a red-faced man—such a red face!
—and Fred used to say you drank too much."

"Fred was always as fond of me as I am of
him," said the doctor, smiling. "But Fred was
right."

"You wore black trousers that bulged dread-
fully at the knees, and a coat that never—whether you walked or stood or sat—hung anyhow
but in bumps and folds. Your boots were worn
down at the heel, and you had a horrid black
waistcoat which was frayed at the pockets."

"Very likely," said Dr. Chacomb. "The
pockets were worn by searching for the coins
which were not there. Those devils of pockets!
I remember them, too. They were my purse,
and the reverse of the purse that Peter Schlemyl
got—"

"Who was Peter Schlemyl?"

"I forget now, except that he sold his shadow, and that he got instead of it a purse, out
of which you could take as much money as
you pleased, without putting any in. Now, you
could put as much as you liked into my pockets,
and there never was anything there. The gold
changed into silver, the silver into copper, and

the copper into nothing at all. But pray go on
with your description. It grows interesting."

"I think I have finished. Stay—you had
immense red hands. I used to wonder how it
would feel to have hands of such an enormous
size. Your hair was thick and matted; your lips
were very large, I remember, and very red; you
had great black eyebrows, and your eyes were
fierce and strong—they seemed to take in everything, and to want to order everybody about.
Altogether, you were not quite nice, somehow.
Comb Leigh did not suit you."

"Good," said the doctor. "On the whole, it
is a clever portrait. But that was four years
ago. Light the candles, look at me again, and
tell me if the portrait will do now."

"There is only an inch or two of candle left,
and what are we to do for more when these are
gone?" said Adie. "Never mind, we can go to
bed in the dark. There, Dr. Chacomb."

"What do you see now?" asked the doctor.

"No," said Adie, "I will not describe you any
more."

The portrait, indeed, no longer represented
Dr. Joseph Chacomb. His face, lit by the can-

dles, had lost its old red hue, and was now pale, but not pallid; his large eyes—formerly, to the young girl's fancy, so fierce—were softened and grave; above them lay eyelids heavy, as if with thought. His eyebrows were no thicker than is befitting to a man of great mental and physical strength. His lips were large, especially the lower lip; but you may remark the same prominence in that feature in the photograph of nearly every great statesman, lawyer, or preacher. His hair, grown thin at the temples, was strong, closely knitted, and not yet touched with grey—a sturdy crop of brown curls. His large hands, from which he had removed the gloves, were now white and shapely. He was dressed by Poole, in such garments as belong especially to the prosperous physician—a black buttoned frock, and grey trousers in which no trace of Adie's ancient "bulge" was visible. A pair of double eye-glasses in gold hung from his neck.

"Of course I knew," said the girl, "without the candles, that you were greatly changed. I was only talking of what you used to be. You are not offended, are you?"

"Not at all; but I want you to understand all about me, and that very clearly. Look at me again. Am I younger or older than I used to be?"

"Younger, to look at."

"If a man is younger to look at, he is younger in reality. There is no wearing of wigs about me; it is all Nature's handiwork. I am exactly what you see me, and I was exactly four years ago what you knew me then. I ought, by all the rules of life, to be four years worse— fiercer in the face, redder in the eyes, clumsier in the paws; but I am not, you see. I am ten years younger; I am not red-faced at all. You have never asked me what has effected this transformation."

She shook her head.

"I will tell you."

"If it is a story, let me put out the candles. You can talk by the gaslight just as well."

"Rubbish! Let them burn out; I will give you plenty more. Listen to me, child. When the unsuccessful man putteth off his unsuccess, he lays aside his bad habits. Of bad habits come red faces and fierce eyes; of unsuccess come old

coats, down-at-heel boots, and bulgy bags.
Failure in a man is like a fallow soil to the
fields, because it causes all manner of ill weeds
to grow. When you knew me first, I was a
failure; now I am a success."

"I am glad to hear it," said Adie. "I wish
you would teach Fred the way to become a
success."

"Fred! As if any teaching would do him
any good! But have you no curiosity? Do
you not care to ask what I have done?"

"No," said the girl. "Men are always doing
something to make money. It seems to me to
matter very little what they actually do, so long
as they get it, and give it to their daughters."

"There is no critical faculty at all," said the
doctor, "in the feminine mind. If Eve had
only been told not to inquire how Adam made
his money, we should all have been gardening
in Paradise this day. I never did like gardening, for my part, so I am mightily obliged to
Eve. Then, Adie, since you do not ask me, I
must tell you. You have never heard, I suppose, of the Royal Hospital for Gout, supported
by voluntary contributions?"

Adie shook her head.

"You see," she said, "I never had gout. It comes of eating and drinking too much, I believe. We are not at all likely—Marion and I—to get gout. Perhaps Fred may get it some day."

"I am its Founder," he said, with pride. "Of all my projects, it is the only one which I have pulled off. The rest, poor innocents, perished unborn. But one is enough. I founded it. Alone I did it. I hired the building, got my secretary, and organized my management. It is now a flourishing institution. I am the chief consulting physician. We appeal especially— it is a stroke of real genius this, if you could only understand it—to those who have never had the disease. The funds come in, and my fortune is made."

"Do you mean that you take all the money that people send?" asked Adie, in her innocence.

"No, my dear young lady. That would be an elementary proceeding unworthy of my genius, and leading to unpleasant interviews with the magistrates. My fortune is built upon my reputation, and that is based upon my hos-

pital.   I am now the leading specialist on gout.
Dr. Porteous, of Savile-row, pretends to be my
superior; but you will not believe that."

"Very well," said Adie, innocently; "I will
not."

"My income is over four thousand a year,
and it goes on increasing like a snowball.   You
understand so far?

"Yes.   You have got more money than you
know what to do with."

"Not quite.   However, this is what I am
coming to.   I want to marry Marion.   If she
will have me, I will take you away to a pleasant
house at the other end of town.   You shall have
a carriage to ride in.   Do you hear?"

"Ah!" cried the girl, her colour flushing.

"You shall leave this, place, and go into the
country, to the seaside—wherever you please.
You shall have money to spend, and as much as
you want.   You shall associate with ladies and
gentlemen again.   You shall dress as a young
lady of your beauty—you know what a pretty
girl you are, Adie—ought to dress.   You shall
have lessons in all young ladies' accomplishments.   You shall pick up the threads of your

life where you dropped them four years ago, only they shall lead to a life broader and more famous, and fuller in enjoyment. You shall belong to the world that you envy. Only you must help me."

"How can I help you?" she asked, with lips apart and brightened eyes.

"Will you if you can?"

"Will I not? Would I not do anything, anything to get out of this dreadful place, and feel once more that to-morrow's food at least is ready and certain? You know that Marion is reserved. I cannot go to her and say, 'Marion, you are a great goose to refuse the good luck that offers for both of us.' If I were even to hint at it, things would be worse than ever. There must be no appearance of my helping, even if I see a way."

The doctor considered.

"Time is precious to a man when he is on the verge of fifty. There are only ten years more of enjoyment before him. I want to marry at once, Adie, and waste none of those valuable years. First of all, however, I must help you. Don't be proud, child. You have no money?"

"Not one penny. I told you so."

"Then you must not refuse to take some. I suppose you keep house while Marion paints?"

"Yes."

"I think you had better not let her know, if you can help it, that I have given you anything. Only take care that you always have plenty to eat. See, here are five pounds for you and Marion, for your housekeeping. I put the money into your hands on the condition that you do not give it to your brother to waste. Spend it on yourselves. Let Marion, if you like, believe that it is careful housekeeping. And as to helping me, you can only do it by letting Marion feel, day by day, the misery of poverty."

Adie considered.

"That may seem cruel, but it is really kind. As soon as Marion begins to realize that her compliance means your restoration to the world of respectability, she will comply."

"But about Fred. You will help the poor boy too, won't you?"

"I am not at all obliged to provide for Fred," said the doctor; "but I will do what I can for him. Fred shall not be forgotten; that is all I

can promise on his account. It is you that I
should like to see happy and well provided for,
my dear child. I want to have you with us for
a year or two before you marry and leave us;
to see you enjoy yourself at balls and operas
and theatres; to bring a little more plumpness
to those fair cheeks of yours."

The doctor had got her hand in his, was
bending his face to hers, and you might almost
have thought by the look of his eyes that
he was making love to her. But he was not:
it was only a way that he had, and the natural pleasure which every well-regulated male
mind feels at having a girl's soft hand in his
own.

"I should like, my girl, to make you happy,
as well as Marion. Are you afraid of me?"

"But Marion must be made happy first," said
Adie. "How do I know that you will be kind
to her, as well as to me? Marion is not so easy
to get on with as I am; she takes everything so
seriously, you know. And, besides, it is not me
you want to marry, but Marion."

"If you are not afraid of me, why should
Marion be? If you would not laugh at me, I

would tell you that I love her. I do indeed. I
have always loved her."

"Have you? It seems very funny that you
should love Marion. You are such very different people. Perhaps, though, that is the reason why you love her. But I do not want to
laugh."

"What would you say if I told you I loved
you, Adie?"

"I cannot imagine such a thing to happen at
all," she replied. "It is no use speculating.
One thing you may be quite certain of: if you
were Blue Beard himself, and I were only going
to be the last wife but one, I would marry you
if you asked me, to get out of this doleful life.
Yes, I would. And if I were Marion, I would
marry any one who would give us enough to
eat. If I were Beauty herself, I would marry
the Beast with pleasure, if he would give me
proper dresses and the things that make life
comfortable as well. I would do anything
for more money, Dr. Chacomb—anything, I
declare."

"Have patience a little, Adie," said the doctor, smoothing her hair with his palm. "Wait

till I bring home Marion for my bride, and you shall have all you want. I am not quite Blue Beard, nor yet quite the Beast; but tell me," he added, sentimentally, "would you mind having me for your brother-in-law?"

"Not a bit," said Adie, truthfully. "I should rather like it, I think. You are the only gentleman we know, and I am sick of starving. Fred never does anything for us; I can do nothing for myself. What are we to look forward to? You are quite sure you will not do anything horrid after you are married? Because, you know, I should feel miserable all my life if poor Marion were made unhappy through me."

"Trust me, Adie," said Dr. Chacomb; "and help me if you can. See, you have forgotten the money."

Adie took up the five glittering sovereigns, and held them in her hands, holding them to the light with an admiration that had a sort of tremor in it. She had never before had so much money given her all at once, and the gold represented a boundless vista of rich and luxurious probability.

"It seems wrong, somehow," she said, "to take your money. Suppose nothing comes of it, after all. Suppose Marion will not be persuaded to marry you. Suppose you reproach me for doing nothing. Mind, I cannot promise much. I will do what I can, because I think it is the best thing for us all, not because I want it by itself, and very much, to happen. And you will perhaps turn round then, and say I took the money from you."

"Joseph Chacomb, Adrienne Revel"—in less prosperous days he would have said "Joe Chacomb"—"Joseph Chacomb has faults. He is sometimes called overbearing, chiefly by his enemies; but do not forget that he comes, like yourself, of gentle blood. We are the Chacombs of Chacomb. My cousin Chauncey, poor fellow, and I are now alone to represent the family, unless Gerald turns up again. You may at least trust Joseph Chacomb to be a gentleman."

"Good night, then, Dr. Chacomb, and thank you."

"Hush! I hear Marion's step."

The pair separated guiltily, Adie slipping the

money into her pocket. The man's ear was quicker than the girl's, for immediately afterwards the door opened, and Marion Revel came in.

Four years of hard and careworn struggles have placed their mark upon her. She was little more than a girl when we saw her last, with the buoyancy of girlhood still on her; she appears a woman of thirty now, by her wasted cheeks and her faded look. She is dressed, like Adie, in a cheap stuff, cut and trimmed by her sister in the fashion, so that she might not look dowdy. Her gloves are worn and mended. She has something of the air, without the meekness induced by incessant obedience, of a nun or a Sister of Mercy. Under her arm she carries a parcel, which Adie recognizes, with a heart-sinking, as the packet of drawings she took away with her in the morning.

"You, Dr. Chacomb?"

She put down her drawings, and held out her hand, with a smile which suddenly brought back all her youth. She was only twenty-seven, after all—that halting-place in the growth of

womanhood where youth and beauty meet, the
time when a girl may be at her sweetest and
freshest, or may be *blasée* and worn out. Marion should have been at her sweetest and
freshest, but for the sad reasons of hard work,
anxiety, and insufficient food. The Princess
of Fairy-land can live on nothing; her tears
nourish her, as they did the Psalmist; her
hopes sustain her; her faith cheers her. In
Real-land the Princess grows pale and weak
when she has not a good dinner every day.
In her distress she lives chiefly on tea and
bread. After a while her spirits fail, her faith
declines—all for the want of proper food. Ra-
belais makes great Gaster the first Master of
Arts, the first great inventor, the deviser of
every art; he should have gone farther still,
and made him the nourisher, the support, stay,
prop, and comfort of love.

"You, Dr. Chacomb! It is a long time since
you came to see us last."

"It is not my fault if I do not come oftener,"
said the doctor. "You have only to say that
you like to see me."

"Of course we like to see you. You are our

last link with the past. If it were not for you to remind us that things were really what we remember, Adie and I should get to believe that we had been all our lives in Lowland-street."

"Yes," said Adie; "sometimes I believe we were. Comb Leigh seems a dream."

She took her sister's packet of drawings, and looked inquiringly.

Marion shook her head.

"I have had a weary day, dear, and very little luck. Mr. Burls swore, in his pretty fashion, over the forest birds, and would not look at the wild flowers. But he has promised to get me some work, doing curtains and backgrounds for a portrait painter, if he can. Then I walked over Waterloo Bridge, and saw Mr. Hermann. I think I dislike him worse than Mr. Burls. He was not in his office, and so I came home. Oh, I forgot to say that I waited for five hours at Mr. Burls's, and began to copy a head for him. So I have not wasted the day. And Adie—?" She looked wistfully at her sister.

"I have been alone all day. At six o'clock I left off work, and went downstairs to have tea with Mr. Owen. Winifred came home early. Then Dr. Chacomb came in, and we have been talking. Let me take the poor pictures, dear. I wish Mr. Burls had his head between them, so that I could squeeze it—like this—to a jelly, the horrid man, for swearing. I have promised to see Winifred again this evening," she added, mendaciously. "I will leave you with Dr. Chacomb. Good night, doctor."

"Why do you reproach me with not coming, Miss Revel?" he began. "You know the reason."

"There is no reason," she returned, with a little bitterness. "That is no reason at all. You asked what you knew you never could have; you were foolish — or were you kind? Perhaps you only thought of my happiness, to ask. But you might have known—surely, no one could have known better than yourself—how utterly impossible it was. You promised never to allude to it again."

Dr. Chacomb waved his hand. Nothing more strongly marked the difference between the man now and the man of four years ago than the attitude in which he stood, the air with which he listened, the gesture with which he received the young lady's appeal. Everything betrayed the man of self-possession, of experience, of reserve—the man accustomed to converse on equal terms with those whom a former generation called persons of quality. Now, anybody can be a gentleman of Bloomsbury, of Camberwell, or even of Islington; but it requires some adaptability to put on the air of the middle-aged gentleman of Belgravia. As for the young gentleman of that district, he is born, not made, like the poet, and cannot be imitated. Those who attempt to copy him are like Icarus, who flew too high; and, like him, they fall and perish miserably.

Four years ago, Dr. Chacomb would have been nervous, shy, and ill at ease with ladies; four years ago, with Marion herself he found himself expressing sentiments that smacked of Bohemia in the language of Bohemia; four years ago, the gifts and graces of life were like the latter letters of the alphabet to the algebra lecturer, his unknown quantities. He is polished now: the same man still, but with the outward veneer of self-control. What *docs* it matter, perhaps, how selfish, how cruel, how licentious your disposition may be, provided the veneer is thick enough to prevent anybody finding it out? And if even your wife never discovers the faults that lie seething beneath, if her only complaint of you is that you show—being at heart a Blue Beard for philandering, a Nero for cruelty, and a Louis Quatorze for selfishness—a certain lack of sympathy, a strange reserve as to things holy and good, why, civilization has done something. Success had civilized the doctor.

He waved his hand with a gentle sweep of deprecation.

"Nay," he said, "I hardly promised never to open the subject again. On the contrary, I came to open it to-night."

"You have news?"

"None from Gerald. No line has come from him since he left England. I have told already what we know. We traced him to the Cape; from Cape Town to the Trans Vaal Territory; then we lost sight of him. I have no news to give you of Gerald. Believe me, Miss Revel, in spite of my own hopes, I am sorry to have nothing to tell you—of him."

"I believe you, Dr. Chacomb. You are a true friend."

"I would have shown that a long time ago, had either you or Gerald told me at the time of my cousin's strange hallucination, and what he said. He has it still, Miss Revel. I heard to-day from the person who has charge of him. The belief is on him stronger than ever. In other respects he is calm, rational, and consistent; in this alone he is mad, hopelessly mad. He believes that he murdered your father."

"At least he hated him," said Marion. "There is no delusion there."

"Yes, he hated him; he hates his memory still. But that is nothing; it is all part of his madness. Forget Chauncey Chacomb, Miss Revel! The poor lunatic never did your father any harm, save in thought. He is quite innocuous; and if you were to go and see him, he would probably sit down and cry."

"I could not bear to see him."

"But never mind Chauncey Chacomb; I came here to-night on a different errand. I came to ask you, Miss Revel, once more how long you are going to mourn over a lost love."

"Always, Dr. Chacomb."

"It is not as if you had been married. Even
then a widowhood of four years in one so young
would have been a great deal to give."

There was an innate coarseness of feeling
in the man that success and veneer could not
wholly hide, and which made itself felt in such
speeches as these. You know how vases of a
debased period still proclaim the vulgarity of
their form, however they are painted or gilded.
Dr. Joseph Chacomb considered Marion's ob-
stinacy as something conventional and affected,
like the prolongation of her mourning by a widow
who ought rather to rejoice over her eman-
cipation. What was the good of it? Fish swim
in the sea as good as those which lie in the fish-
monger's window. If Gerald was gone, there were
other lovers to be had, notably himself. It irritated him, this constancy. And yet had he been
asked to give up Marion, had he been told that
there were plenty of girls as good as Marion in
the world, he would have laughed at the impos-
sibility of finding one that could be to him what
Marion might be. He really loved her. Perhaps, too, there was a little pity in his feeling

towards Marion. She had been so happy, and was now so poor. Quite selfish men very often nurse the luxury of pity with great enjoyment, and even endeavour, when possible, to combine relief to the unfortunate with more enjoyment for themselves. If, for instance, Dr. Chacomb had come across Jephthah's daughter lamenting among the mountains, he would have been moved to the deepest pity by her beauty and her distress combined; while ugly virgins in basketfuls might have wept without attracting his sympathy. Most likely, after a little consideration, he would have proposed to remove the cause of her tears by an immediate elopement and secret marriage at the nearest sacred grove or high-place of Baal.

"A very great deal to give," he went on. "You are young, but you will not always be young. You have given already to the memory of that poor boy the best years of your life. Be reasonable, Marion."

"I try to be reasonable; but it must be in my own way."

"I came to see you to-night," he went on, "in order to make one more appeal to your common

sense. See, now," he said, with a little dropping in his voice—it was remarkable that he did
not take her hand as he had taken Adie's—"see,
Marion, you do not absolutely hate me."

"Indeed, I do not hate you in the least.
Quite the contrary. I am always very glad to
see you."

"There it is, then. Half the battle is won if
you have overcome your dislike to me. I know
that when you first made my acquaintance, appearances were against me. I was horribly poor;
I was desperately in debt; and I had fallen into
coarse habits. All that is altered now. There
is nothing to prevent any lady from marrying
me."

She shook her head and answered nothing.
It was the second time, and she knew what
would follow.

"Then it is surely something that I am getting rich more rapidly than I could ever have
hoped or expected. There is no profession in
which money accumulates faster than mine, once
you make a start. I've made a splendid start."

"I'm very glad indeed—for your sake."

"Be glad for your own, Marion. I wish I was

a younger and a more eloquent man, to persuade you the better. Be glad for your own; I want you for my wife. In all the world I don't think I have a single friend—not a man, woman, or child to whom I can tell whatever I have on my mind. When you are struggling, it doesn't matter; but when you are rich and comfortable, you want a companion. It is not good—Scripture warrant—for a man to be alone. When I sit at home, after a dinner that a duchess—yes, a duchess—would enjoy, I cannot drink a bottle of port as I used to four years ago, because I must consider my nerves for the next day's work. I hardly can smoke now. I don't care to read. And thus it is that I want a wife to talk to me. Be my wife, Marion."

She shook her head again silently.

"I will be kind to you; I will indeed. You shall never hear a harsh word from me. I will consider your wishes in everything; you shall have the direction and ordering of the whole house. I shall be contented to make money for you to spend, provided I can only see you my wife."

He began to tick off on his fingers the special

4—2

advantages she might derive from a union with himself.

"Look at yourself, now—toiling and moiling for a miserable pittance, and putting money into other people's hands. What have you had to eat to-day? Next to nothing. Adie told me. You have actually suffered privation — you. What will your work lead to? More misery, more starvation, more wretchedness for you and your sister. I offer to take you—and her—out of it all."

He ticked this off as a telling point, and went on again after a moment's consideration. The man was tremendously in earnest; but each sentence jarred upon the girl's nature, and made compliance with his wish the more impossible.

"Adie, now. Do you think it right and proper that she should be living in this style, brought up as she was? She is twenty years of age, as beautiful as Helen of Troy, and full of longings for the good things of the world. Remember that it will be your own fault if she continues to go on like this. Why, I've known girls, out of desperation"—he stopped for a moment—

"do all sorts of things. Marion, think of Adie before you give me up."

Tick the second. Then he played what he thought a stronger card.

"There is your brother Fred. He has been loafing about town for four years, living on your exertions. Now I tell you candidly and honestly that he will never do any work at all. He does not want any. I know the London loafer. Every day makes him fonder of the billiard tables, and less inclined to work. Fred *couldn't* do any work if he had any to do; it is impossible for him now, even if it was possible for him four years ago. You will have to go on working for him as well as for your sister. You will see him descend lower and lower. He is already at a tolerably low level. You will watch the last pretence of trying for work disappear, and the last scruple at depending upon your exertions; you will see the very last flickering spark of his honour die."

"Dr. Chacomb!"

It was a good blow, and he repeated it, thinking he would drive the nail home.

"You will see the last flickerings of his honour

die out bit by bit. He will lose all that you have admired in him. Well if he does not bring disgrace upon your name. I offer you relief from this infliction. I will myself provide for your brother."

The girl made him no reply, but her head sank lower.

"Gerald is dead," he went on—"of that be very certain. Gerald is either dead or he has forgotten you, and his father, and the past, all of us together. Do you think that he would not have written had he been alive? Do you still believe that on the word of a madman, accepting a wild statement which he never even tried to question or to prove, he would have stayed away for four years, and made no sign? Why, anything might happen. His father's life—Chauncey has got heart disease—hangs upon a thread; the estates might come to me. You might have married some one else. Nonsense! Gerald is dead, or Gerald has ceased to think about you."

"If he has ceased to think about me, that is no reason why I should cease to think about him," said Marion. "If he is dead, let me mourn for him still."

"No, Marion." He lowered his voice, and his eyes, under the rolls of fat eyelids, assumed a softer light. "No, Marion, mourn no more. You have had enough of misery and sorrow; let the dead bury the dead. The memory of your father's death must not cloud the whole of your life. There has been too much mourning. Come back to the world, and take your place among the ladies of the world, the sweetest and best of them all. I swear there is no one like you, Marion—no one among the countesses and people—wherever I go. Come out of this dreary and starving den, where you lie hidden and forgotten. Good God! to think that you should dream of going on here, and like this, for ever!"

"Not for ever," said Marion—"not for ever. There *is* an end appointed."

"Yes, and it is appointed by *me*," said the doctor, with an earnestness which perhaps redeemed the audacity of the statement. "Be my wife, Marion, and all shall be well with you. I am hungering and thirsting for you. Come to me, and I will make you happy. Come to me, and your sister shall be happy. Come to me,

and I will rid you of that idle, good-for-nothing
rascal, your brother."

As he spoke, the door opened, and the idle
rascal himself appeared. He had a cigar in his
mouth, and stood for a moment looking at the
doctor, as if uncertain what to say. He lifted
his hat, took the cigar from his lips, and stepped
in with an air of easy dignity, such as might
belong to Alcibiades in his early days of success,
wealth, and an easy conscience. The doctor saw
with admiration how handsome the young man
was, with what a fearless confidence he held his
head, how clear and honest was the look in his
eyes, how frank and gallant was the pose of his
figure. He was well dressed, too, and wore a
hat of the newest and glossiest. It was not till
after he got home that Dr. Chacomb was able to
put it to himself with indignation how, while his
sisters were starving, their brother was so fat and
well-looking; how he could afford cigars whose
perfume spoke of nothing less than sixpence
a-piece; and how an idler and a loafer had the
impudence to look so independent.

"You will rid my sister of the idle rascal, her
brother," said Mr. Frederick Revel, quietly. "It

is not the first time, sir, that you have volunteered your advice; but I hope—I believe, it is the first time that you have openly insulted my sister by abusing her brother. Leave the room, sir!"

It is one of the easiest things in the world to say; but unless the words take effect instantly, the order has to be repeated.

Dr. Chacomb looked at the young man as if he had not spoken; or, rather, he looked through him, fixing his eyes thoughtfully on a sketch upon the wall behind him.

"Leave the room, Dr. Chacomb, unless you wish to go through the window."

"Fred!" cried Marion. "Dr. Chacomb—for Heaven's sake!"

"Miss Revel," said the latter, "I will call and see you again, when we shall not be interrupted. There will be no going through the window, so far as I am concerned."

"Understand, sir," cried Fred, fiercely—no one, not even the laziest of *lazzaroni*, likes to be called an idle rascal—"that I object to your coming to this house at all."

"I thought," said the doctor, with a smile,

"that the lodgings were taken, and—and, in fact, paid for by the exertions of your sister. Perhaps I was wrong."

"I object to your presence here; I will not have it. My sisters are under my care and protection."

He looked for the moment as if it really was by the labour of his hands that they were housed and maintained.

"Your care and protection?" Dr. Chacomb shook his head slowly. "They have done great things for the young ladies. They provide your sisters with good lodgings, companionship of their own class, plentiful food, and abundance of pocket money—"

The young man interrupted him with an impatient gesture.

"Your sisters ought to be, and are, no doubt, infinitely obliged to you. Mr. Frederick Revel, do not talk nonsense. You must try bounce with other people. Remember, sir, the time will come when even the self-sacrifice of a sister will fail you, when the devotion that has kept you in idleness so long will be tired out, and when your own petty tricks to keep up the appearance of a gentleman will break down. Miss Revel, you will not forget what I said. You have but to order me, and I will free you of the burden"—he spoke very slowly, shaking his forefinger at Fred—"of this idle, good-for-nothing, spendthrift brother of yours."

Marion held out her hand. Frederick threw himself into a chair, with a futile effort to preserve his dignity.

"Do not," Marion murmured—"do not be hard on poor Fred. We are as we are—what God made us, I suppose. And—and—Dr. Chacomb, do not desert us. Try to be kind *to them*, and forget me."

CHAPTER III.

THE starving poet whom Pope in England, Boileau, Saint Amant, and Regnier in France, have held up to the derision of posterity, lived in a garret, sometimes sharing his pallet (whatever a pallet may be) with a fellow in starving aspiration. Many an unfortunate young gentleman, with a turn for imitative scribbling and a capacity for idleness, has imagined that to be uncomfortably poor and to live in a garret are necessary conditions of the poetic life in its embryo. This belief sweetens the water of affliction, and spreads the crust of poverty with Sicilian honey. It is, therefore, useful. Chatterton, Savage, Béranger, Mürger — the name is legion of those who have lived at the top of the house in their youth, though not all

have survived that period and come down. But
there comes a time when the imagination takes
sober tints, and expectation of success changes
into certainty of defeat. Then the poet curses
his garret, with all that thereto appertains—
the narrow limits of its four walls, the stairs
which lead to it, the wind which blows down
the chimney, the wretched furniture which helps
to make it unlovely, the prospect from the
chimney tops, his own bad luck in being born
a bard.

Mr. Richard Carew—whose character might
be gathered from the simple fact that his friends
always called him Dicky and nothing else, so
that had there been a thousand Richards in
the field, or rather at the public-house bar,
there would have been but one Dicky—was
arrived at the time in the life of a genius when
the early hopes have been blighted, and disappointment has been accepted. He is thirty
years of age, and is certainly as poor as when
he began, perhaps poorer, because his wardrobe is more scanty. He has been in the profession for ten years, during which time the
heartless world has allowed him to remain in

the garret where first he slung his hammock.
He has now—the bitterest blow of all—come
to disbelieve in his own genius. *He has left off
trying.* That is fatal. So long as you continue
to write there is hope—*qui scribit laborat;*
glimpses of true art are caught by him who is
always copying or endeavouring to draw, however thin be the vein and Minerva unwilling;
felicities of expression come of their own accord to him who continuously writes, like a
happy combination of colours to him who
shakes up the kaleidoscope long enough.
Dicky, however, has for the last three or four
years forgotten the ambition which led him
to abandon the usher's desk at a Devonshire
provincial academy, and change it for the garret
of a genius. He has sold the little library of
great authors whom once he studied. He reads
no more except to copy; he writes no more,
except to perform, with as little trouble as may
be, the daily task.

The place is in Lowland-street, two doors
from No. 15. The garret already alluded to
is not the apartment one would choose for
luxury. It is long and narrow, with a sloping

roof. It is furnished with a contempt of luxury worthy of Diogenes. Although the residence of a literary man, there are no books in it; and although the home of a genius, there are no sheets of writing-paper on the one table. Perhaps, however, he works with his brain. The place is low and close, in spite of the chimney, which acts as a ventilator. It contains a chair or two, a chest of drawers, a table, and an iron bedstead, whose sheets and pillows are crying aloud for a bath. It is eleven in the morning, and the tenant of the room is lying on his back in the bed, with his hands joined under his head, and his eyes wide open.

"I suppose," he growls, "that the longer I stay in bed, the hungrier I shall get. Why can't a man sleep it off?"

He got out of bed with an air of disgust, and began to dress. Dicky Carew boasted a shock crop of red hair, a face which would have been a figure-head of health but for the redness of his nose, and a profusion of whiskers which stood out on either cheek, imparting to what Nature intended for the emblem of meekness the look of extreme ferocity.

If it were fair, which it certainly is not, to reveal the secrets of a gentleman's toilet, one might illustrate the simple severity of Mr. Carew's manner by one or two striking particulars. Some children of the present luxurious generation, for instance, would be too proud to wash their only pocket handkerchief with their own hands. Dicky was not. He whistled, indeed, over his task, with the ease and freedom which a happy conscience imparts to an habitual duty. It might even have been objected that he spent more time in washing the linen than in washing himself.

"The consumption of soap is awful," he murmured, looking at the wasted cake. "I must really get to the Museum early to-morrow"— a *non sequitur* at first sight as profound as the celebrated typical case of Stoney Stratford, except to the initiated few.

A daily inspection of his wardrobe was necessitated by reason of its great scantiness; for Dicky, like Diogenes, St. Francis, or St. Anthony, scorned to spend money on raiment and fine linen. Still, it is known to all that seams will separate in which we have too long placed our trust; buttons will fail on which, forgetful of the mortality of perishable things, we have relied too confidently; edges in conspicuous places will fray and fringe.

He looked first at the heels of his boots, and groaned aloud; they were worn to their junction with the upper leathers. The thought forced itself upon his mind that in a day or two it would be absolutely necessary to have them heeled, or even to reject them altogether.

"I've read of a Frenchman," he said, "who discovered that his boots wore out on the pavements of Paris as fast under a Republic as an Empire. I believe the free institutions of England are more fatal than either to the heels of boots. Where can I get the money for new heels? I wish there was another Revolution."

He observed that his trousers showed signs of unforeseen decay about the knees, and his heart sank.

"Show me," he said, almost fiercely, "the capitalist who can afford two new pairs of second-hand machine-made reach-me-downs in a single winter. Where is he, I say? Produce him."

His coat, which was originally a black walking coat of fashionable cut, had been for some months slowly turning green. Dicky laid it over a chair where it could catch the full effect of the sunshine, and retired a few steps to watch the effect.

"It's beautiful," he said, "regarded as an effort of Nature in her most sympathetic mood, and as something to talk about for people who've got what art critics call the 'vivid passion of sight.' The coat is better altogether than Joseph's. No such depth of light and shadow could be got out of a coat of many colours. You want a single shade, such as green, growing out of an originally black ground, but in different gradations; a touch of green on a foundation of black, in places where the nap gets rubbed off between the shoulders—those Museum chairs do wear the shoulders shamefully; where it buttons across the chest, a pale green with a lustrous shimmer; where it's simply shiny, the right cuff for example, it's like a piece of imitation Bohemian glass; the deeper artistic feeling comes out in the folds of the tail as it hangs gracefully from the figure. If all the world were artists; if everybody had the æsthetic eye of a— a—Nicolas Poussin, one would wear that coat with pleasure and pride. As it is, I should like to have a new one, and I can't get it."

He investigated his pockets one after the other. There was a penny in one, some loose tobacco in another, a pipe in a third, a pencil with some paper for notes in a fourth.

"I have heard—or did I read it once when I used to read books?—of a man who found a half-sovereign in his waistcoat pocket. Perhaps —no, there's no half-sovereign there. As for breakfast, I must go without. I shall be able to raise a couple of shillings from old Lilliecrip, I dare say. That will carry me through the day. Eleven o'clock, Lilliecrip at twelve, writing till three—nothing to eat till half-past, even if I do get the two shillings.

"Now if I had only not gone to the Harmonic last night—only not gone—my head would have been clearer this morning, and there would have been five shillings in my pocket instead of a penny. What's the good of a penny?"

He took it out and held it up disconsolately.

"A bronze penny. In the good old days, a

5—2

penny had its value; it was a good lump of
copper; you could buy things with it. England
has never been merry England since copper
pennies went out."

The clock chimed the half-hour. He took
his hat.

"I may as well go," he said. "There is not
much to make one linger in this retreat."

He twirled his hat thoughtfully.

"What a hat for a gentleman and a genius!
It was a Lincoln and Bennett once, and figured
on the stage. I believe Toole played in it. Ah,
it looked very different in its youth, I dare say.
It was glossy and black, for certain; now it's
shiny and brown. It used to be brushed regu-
larly, no doubt; now it's a very dangerous thing
to brush it. I am sure it must have had a stiff
brim both before and behind; now it's so limp
that it can't be taken off except from the top,
like a priest's biretta. It was once of fashionable build—Lord! Lord! who would think so
now? I should date that hat, I think, at 1860,
or thereabouts."

He put it on his head, a little to one side—
which gives, as every one knows, from the com-

mander-in-chief to yesterday's recruit, a smart and even a rakish air; put up his note-book, felt for his pencil and keys, took from the corner a coloured cane—quite a gentlemanly cane, which was the pride of his heart, and which he handled as delicately as a Life Guardsman on a Sunday afternoon—and went downstairs.

On the second floor he stopped, looked doubtful, shook his head, and tapped at the door. A voice replied, and he entered.

"You needn't trouble to ask me this morning, Mr. Carew," said a querulous voice; "I've got no money to lend, or to give, or to throw away."

The voice came from an easy-chair by the fireside, where a very old woman sat propped up with pillows.

"My dear madam," said Dicky, with the sweetest manner in the world, "I am sure I never thought of borrowing even a sixpence of you; I am only anxious to repay you the small sums which—let me see"—he produced his note-book—"it was—how much was it?"

"Three pound four and tenpence."

"Let us say, between friends, and to make it

round money, three pounds five," said Dicky, making a careful note of it. "My aunt from Westmoreland is coming to town, I expect, in a day or two. She will—"

"I don't believe you've got an aunt in Westmoreland at all," returned the lady in the chair. "Whenever you owe me money it's your aunt in Westmoreland."

"My *dear* madam," Dick replied, with unction, "is it possible you mistrust *me*, your old friend, Richard Carew? You must be unwell; you suffer this morning, poor dear. Let me shake up the pillows." He crossed the room delicately, and adjusted the cushions of the great chair in which the old woman sat propped. "Poor dear soul! And yet there's the look of youth in her eyes still."

"Go away, do," said the old woman. "My granddaughter told me when she went to rehearsal this morning not to lend you another sixpence if you was to beg for it on your bended knees."

"I did not come to borrow," said Mr. Carew. "Can we not be disinterested for a moment in this world? You will not deny—come, now, deny it if you can—that your eyes once played the very devil with the fellows."

"Perhaps they did, Mr. Carew, perhaps they did," she replied, twinkling and mollified. "But long ago. Lord bless me, I played with the infant Roscius at Drury Lane: I was the Player Queen to his Hamlet. Eyes? Ay, to be sure. Why not? Fellows were fellows, then, too."

"They were," said Dicky; "I've read of them. Gad, ma'am, I was born too late. Those hands, too. What delicacy in the shaping of the taper fingers! Blood shown in the almond nails—"

"Very likely," said the old lady, looking complacently at her withered old fingers. "My mother was on the stage before me."

"Ah! Possibly—who knows?—Royal blood; pearly nails; pink and rosy palm. Don't think I only come to borrow money, ma'am. When hollow hearts—you remember Byron?"

"I used to know him."

"Happy man! 'When hollow hearts shall wear a mask, will break your own to see, Then, Dudu, let me only ask if that resembles me.'"

He grasped her by the hand, cast one eye on

the mantelshelf in hopes that a casual shilling
might, as had happened once or twice already,
be lying ready for the borrower's hand, and left
her, creeping out with sympathetic tread.

Outside the door he winked and smiled, and
shook his head a great many ways.

"Breaking up at last, poor old girl! Many's
the pound I've had out of her. Memory seems
going at last. On Sunday it was four pounds
eight and sixpence. She's forgotten one pound
three, as near as I calculate it. Now, that's all
clear gain."

On the ground floor he tapped again. There
was no answer, so he opened the door uninvited,
and looked in. A comely woman of forty-five
was busily ironing, crooning a tune all to herself
the while. She looked up in his face with a
pleasure which was quite unaffected and real.

"Why, Mr. Carew," she said, "I thought you
were out and about hours ago. I haven't seen
you, not these three days."

"I have been composing, Mrs. Medlar," he
replied, "since daybreak."

He pressed his hand upon his forehead and
sighed heavily.

"Lor! and poetry too, I dare say."

"Poetry it was," said the mendacious one.

"Do you "—Mrs. Medlar sat down before the fire with the hot iron in her hand, occasionally tapping it with the point of her finger, lest it should take advantage of the position to get cold—"do you feel that it exhausts you very much, Mr. Carew? I have heard now, from a gentleman that used to deal at my husband's shop—poet for a tooth-powder and perfumery in quite a large way of business, he was—that what with the rhymes, and the names, and the ideas, it was sometimes enough to make him feel as if he must take a little something, or drop."

Mr. Carew staggered, but caught the back of a chair for support.

"Those were the lower flights," he said, in a sinking voice. "Efforts like mine, Mrs. Medlar, are attended with more trying consequences. At this moment, I feel, I really do feel, as if I had not even breakfasted. Now you'll laugh at that, I suppose."

This statement, at least, was true.

"Poetry seems like ironing, almost," said the

lady. "You work on and on, never thinking,
and all of a sudden down you drop. I was
just feeling a little faintish myself when you
knocked."

Dicky groaned.

"Those who lead public opinion must suffer,"
he said. "There are martyrs to literature of
whom the world knows nothing."

"Poor dear!" said Mrs. Medlar. "I know
what it is to work, and get the reputation, and
that, and all the while no one thinking of your
poor insides. I've seen my own brother come
home from leading a West-end funeral as limp
as that thread paper, and as green as a cucum-
ber. He was one of them as wants constant
support, little and good. The honour and glory
of the funerals was not enough, he used to say,
to make up for the fatigues and the long waiting.
Some of them took biscuits in their pockets, but
he'd never give in to it—he had that feeling for
the look of things. The sinkin', he used to say,
gave him the real mournful look."

Dicky looked round the room. It was a
comfortable room, combining the requisites of
kitchen, dining-room, and *salon;* for Mrs. Med-

lar was a widow with a property of her own, and of an orderly and saving disposition. But it was not the furniture—for with this Mr. Carew was already tolerably familiar—which attracted his attention so much as the shelves above the sideboard. On the lowest of these was a plate, half covered with a basin; and on this his eyes were riveted.

"Excuse me for interrupting you, Mrs. Medlar," he said, with a winning smile of perfectly disinterested curiosity; "but *is* there—do I see in that plate—sausages? Really, now, they *are* sausages. Do you know, my dear soul, that I feel as if a fried sausage, well browned and crisp, was the one thing that I want at this moment to pull myself together."

"Then," said Mrs. Medlar, rising with alacrity, "why didn't you say so at once? A sausage you shall have, and two if you like."

"Generous heart!" murmured Dicky, taking a seat, and stroking his chin while he gently wagged his head. "O, woman, at the hour of tea, a ministering angel she. My own lines, Mrs. Medlar. I will finish the whole poem when I have time, and dedicate it to you."

"If it was only the hour of tea, Mr. Carew."

By this time the sausages were in the frying-pan. "Only the hour of tea." Evidently her words had a meaning not on the surface.

"Ministering angel! If you were Mrs. Carew, it should never be anything but the hour of tea all day long."

She turned the sausages and looked round at him with a smile. Mrs. Medlar's face was a compound of good-nature and shrewdness. She knew pretty well what her literary friend wanted, and she was resolved to keep a tight hold of it for herself—namely, her little income. She knew, too, that Mr. Carew was at best but a humble member of the profession; she could not but compare his worn and seedy raiment with the gorgeous apparel in which her late husband rejoiced; she saw very well that Dicky was often partially, and even sometimes wholly, in-toxicated; she had, on one lamentable occasion, helped him to bed with her own hands. Now the defunct had never returned the worse for liquor, except on proper and expected occasions, such as an Odd Fellows' feast. It was quite certain, again, that Dicky had no money in the bank. All her notions of things right, things respectable, things becoming, were upset by the behaviour of this Bohemian. And yet she liked him. He came at irregular intervals and made love to her, borrowing half-crowns which he never repaid; he made the most solemn protestations of affection when he was in distress, and in moments—literally moments—of affluence he forgot to tap at her door at dewy morn or balmy eve, and left her as neglected as Horace's Lydia. And yet she liked him: it did her good to have the vagabond with her and to scold him; it soothed her to hear his tale of love, the only thing in which she believed him. He came generally in the evening when he had no money, and therefore nowhere else to go, and sat drinking whatever she gave him—contentedly, it must be owned; for Dicky's tastes were catholic, and so long as the liquid had any, even the least, intoxicating qualities, he was happy in consuming it. They tell a story of a Lincolnshire farmer who was accustomed to get drunk every night off brandy and water, and who paid a visit to a Somersetshire cousin. To his astonishment, the cider offered

for the evening refreshment produced no effect;
and after the twentieth tumbler he was heard
to moan, "This is weary, weary work." Dicky
Carew would never have found any weariness,
provided the right conclusion — the state of
drunkenness, in fact—might be seen in the dim
future. But yet the widow liked him.

"Tea!" she repeated, dishing up. "If I were
to offer you either tea or mild ale at this
moment, which would you take?"

"Generally, I should say tea," said the poet;
"but after my labours of this morning, which
have made me nervous, it would be better for
me to take mild ale."

She gave him a shilling, and pointed to a
jug. He disappeared, and presently returned
with a comfortable head of foam upon the
vessel. She noticed, with a quiet smile, that
he neglected to give her back the change. It
was a forgetful way he had.

He sat down to the sausages while his hostess
cut his bread. A pound of sausages, as every
man knows who has lived in chambers and
had dealings with Mr. Tucker or Mr. Prosser,
consists of six. Mrs. Medlar had fried four.

These rapidly disappeared; but instead of grace after meat, Dicky's eyes wandered from the empty dish to the two remaining sausages, looking as innocent as babies and as attractive as infant pig in their clean white skins. It was a mute appeal, but it was unsuccessful; for Mrs. Medlar, to place herself beyond temptation, put them away on the top shelf.

"Now, Mr. Carew, take your beer. Leave me just one glass for my own dinner, and then you may go away."

He took the jug with both hands, and slowly tilted it upwards. When it finally left his lips —it was always a subject of regret with Dicky that he was obliged to take breath twice in a quart—it was empty. He anticipated any reproaches that might fall from the widow's lips by seizing his hat with one hand, and her own fingers with the other.

"Affectionate and self-denying nature," he murmured, "when we are married—"

"Married, indeed!" said Mrs. Medlar, trying to snatch her hand away, and wounded in her tenderest feelings at the absorption of all the beer. "Married, indeed! When will that be?"

"The days," he continued, "shall be one ever-lasting round of sausages, beer, frying-pans, and ironing. You resemble Diana when you fry, and recall the statues of Juno when you iron. And when you drink beer, I am reminded of Venus, who was born of the foam."

What he meant was not clearly comprehended by Mrs. Medlar; but it was intended, and therefore was taken, for a compliment.

"If you meant it," she said; "but there, you don't. You tell the same tale to a dozen wo-men. As for flattery, I believe you could flatter a donkey's hind leg off. I like a man to be real, I do."

"Flattery! O, Mrs. Medlar—may I say, Al-mina?"—this was her baptismal name. "Almina! 'When hollow hearts shall wear a mask, will break your own to see; Then dearest, pray, your conscience ask, if that takes after me.' I wrote the lines this morning, thinking of you; and yet you talk of flattery. But farewell; when a few more moons have worked their baleful will upon this fragile form and laid it in the dust, you, as well as the nation, my Almina, will know what you have lost. For the sausages," he added, in a tragic voice, pulling his hat as hard over his eyes as the limpness of the brim would allow—"for the sausages and the beer, madam, I thank thee."

"Ah," she said to herself when he was gone, "it's all very well, Mr. Carew; but you don't get over me this way. Before we go to the altar, if ever we do go, I shall make the lawyer tie me up fast, and make no mistake. Let me keep my own to myself, and then we'll see about marrying. I believe he's artful enough to make love to one of the young ladies at No. 15, where he goes every day. He'd better not; if he does, I'll County Court him. He's good company, too. Pity he drinks. But, Lord, after all, it would be a poor tale to drag round with a feller that can't keep out of the public, and only because he's good company."

The object of her thoughts, refreshed and strengthened, was on his way to No. 15.

"It was providential," he said, "quite providential, that I did not get up when I woke up first. At the very best it would have been tea and bread-and-butter with Mrs. Medlar, and now it's been sausages and beer."

Arriving immediately at No. 15, he assumed a businesslike air, straightening his back and throwing his head well up. He proceeded slowly up the stairs to the second floor, at which he knocked, and entered with quite a new manner. Dicky had several at command. With Mrs. Medlar he was the hard-worked, sentimental, struggling man of genius; with the employer to whom he gave a part of every day, he was the careful and mechanical amanuensis; with Marion Revel, whom he adored at a distance, he was the melancholy and disappointed student; with Adie and Winifred, he was the dashing and high-spirited young bachelor; with Fred he put on the semblance of a Lothario and man of fashion in disguise—his seediness was temporary, his pecuniary embarrassments were the result of reckless expenditure, the humility of his position was merely parenthetical; with his companions of the British Museum and the evening harmonic meeting he was a jovial, daredevil fellow, whose spirits were always at fever-heat, likely to stick at nothing, who considered himself the greatest of living writers, though as yet he had failed to convince the world of the fact, and who looked forward to a proud and glorious future. In none of these disguises could he succeed in deceiving a single person except himself, on account of his unfortunate habit of getting drunk whenever he possessed or could borrow the necessary ready money. And when, after the usual amount of gin-and-water, Dicky's brain grew clear, but his power over it weak, so that fiction gave way to reality, he appeared in a uniform, simple, and consistent character: its fidelity of colouring in the less attractive details grew sometimes monotonous, and an excess of repetition was even irksome to his audience: for he then showed himself what he actually was, a good-for-nothing scamp who had once dreamed great things, and failed to accomplish even small things. He had grievances in the shape of *coups manqués*—splendid dreams which had come to nothing. He lamented the past, wept over the present, and groaned at the prospect of the future. Dicky's friends began by laughing at him; they ended by finding him a bore. He had, it is true, one or two redeeming points: he was generous, provided his generosity was not exercised so far as to cause him to give up present enjoyment; he was kind-hearted, inasmuch as, if he were to marry Mrs. Medlar, he would spend her money but not ill-treat her; and he had a touch of humour of a pleasant if a common type.

His income, an extremely precarious one, was derived from two or three sources. He contributed paragraphs, literally at a penny a line, to the *Weekly Intelligence*, a paper with an immense circulation, whose proprietor had narrow views as to the marketable value of literary merit. This paper was remarkable for the bold and startling views it advocated on the subject of religious reform, as well as for a rooted antipathy to the monarchical and aristocratic institutions of the country. He was also connected with a small weekly sheet called the *Christian Clerk*, which was at once Anglican, Evangelical, and Conservative. For this paper he wrote short articles of an improving and constitutional tendency. These he got from the works of a few forgotten divines of the last century preserved in the British Museum. And from the two sources together, taking one week with another, he probably contrived to make as much as seventeen shillings a week. As his lodging only cost him four shillings and sixpence, that left him twelve and sixpence for living, luxuries, and the comforts of life. But he had another resource. I do not mean Mrs. Medlar, who might be counted as a third. On the second floor of No. 15 lived, as has been stated, a certain Mr. Lilliecrip, of eccentric manners and retiring customs. Dicky Carew went daily, excepting Saturdays, to Mr. Lilliecrip's lodgings, and there, closeted with the tenant from twelve to half-past two or three, wrote at his dictation. What he wrote, or what he did there, he was bound, under the most tremendous oaths, and penalties almost Masonic, never to reveal. For the services thus rendered he received the honorarium of fifteen shillings weekly. This, therefore, brought his weekly income available for *la nourriture* to twenty-seven shillings and sixpence. He never bought any clothes unless he was absolutely obliged; and as a gentleman can always get enough to eat, counting breakfast, dinner, and supper, for eighteenpence a day as a maximum, it follows that Dicky had exactly seventeen shillings a week to spend in drink. And he nobly spent it all. He drank in the morning, at noon, and at night. He drank whenever he could. He had been three years with Mr. Lilliecrip, and during the whole of that time that gentleman had never once offered him, Dicky used to reflect with indignation, even so much as a glass of pale ale.

"You are late," said Mr. Lilliecrip, looking at his watch; "a quarter of an hour late, sir, and time presses. Let us begin at once."

CHAPTER IV.

"YOU are late, Mr. Carew," said Mr. Lilliecrip, severely; "a whole quarter of an hour late."

Dicky's employer was sitting at a table, a pile of manuscripts before him, which he was annotating and correcting. He lifted his head, showing a face perfectly pale and colourless. It was a long face, and there was plenty of it, because the cheeks and chin were hairless, while on the lip was a heavy white moustache. His hair was long and silvery white; his features were of a kind you do not easily forget, being straight and regular; his forehead was high, but narrow; the upper part of his nose had that very delicate carving which goes with persons of strong artistic tendencies, but little sympathy; his eyes were clear and bright, but rather shifty.

It was a face still extremely handsome, though its owner was well on the shady side of sixty, and might in youth, when the expression would be a little different, have been of wonderful beauty. But it was a face of which Dicky, at least, was heartily weary. Its changeless set regularity, in which not a wrinkle or a crow's-foot but seemed in its appointed place, was a kind of nightmare to him. He hated this man, who was his chief support; he loathed this daily task of sitting at the table and writing, without being allowed to say a word himself, or to ask a question, at his master's dictation; he kicked against the decrees of Fate which bound him to Mr. Lilliecrip's rooms; he envied those happier brethren who were able to lounge all day in the reading-room of the Museum. But though he dared not rebel openly, in secret he nursed daring plans of revenge, and would imagine, while he was writing, little dramas, in which Mr. Lilliecrip and himself were the only figures. The former was at his mercy; he should implore for pardon—Dicky never clearly made out in his own mind how the situation was to be worked up to—and should be spurned with contumely.

He should pray for a day's grace, and should be reminded bitterly, but with overwhelming dignity, of his bond:—"The bond and no more—give me the bond." He should be dismissed into misery with the mocking laugh of revenge. There was a story which Dicky had once read, of a man who, for some unexplained reason of his own, hounded down and persecuted another, following him from one scene of distress to another, and thence to a worse, with an insatiable thirst of revenge. This story Dicky appropriated to himself, and used to rehearse it mentally while he wrote. His imagination was as active as his brain was lazy; and while his fingers moved mechanically, whole dramas were working themselves out in his mind, consisting entirely of separate *tableaux* without any connecting plot.

"Come," said Mr. Lilliecrip, "let us go on."

Dicky took up his pen, adjusted the blotting pad, and waited.

Mr. Lilliecrip slowly rose, and began to walk up and down the room with hands behind his back. Dicky recommenced the melodrama of revenge where he had left it off the day before;

but his eye, as mild as that of a milch cow, only showed habitual attention to the words for which he waited, while his fingers expressed by their attitude an eagerness to begin, almost bordering on enthusiasm.

The Hermit was dressed in a long, grey, cashmere dressing-gown, which reached to his heels, and was tied round the waist by means of a bright crimson silk scarf. Falling open, it disclosed a shirt front of irreproachable fit and brilliant whiteness, set with small diamond studs; his neck was adorned with a collar, in which was a tiny black ribbon in the neatest of bows; his hands were small and white—the hands of a gentleman. As he passed at each turn before the looking glass on the mantelshelf, he stopped and looked at himself with the complacency of self-satisfaction. His figure was tall, thin, and stooping; his expression was cold, self-contained, and repellent of familiarity; his step was firm and elastic.

"Where did I leave off yesterday?" he said. "Let me consider."

"We were with William the Fourth, sir," said his secretary.

"With William the Fourth. I was engaged on that part of my personal recollections which are concerned with William the Fourth. Yes, yes."

He looked in the glass, and carefully brushed off a tiny speck of dust which had settled on his nose. Then he resumed his walk, thinking. Dicky sat motionless, pen in hand. Once, two years before, he had ventured to blow his nose during a period of silence, but had been so pointedly invited to disturb Mr. Lilliecrip outside, and on his way up, rather than in the room, that he dared no longer so much as to cough.

For fourteen long years this man had never left the two rooms in which he lived; for fourteen years he had lived a perfectly lonely and solitary life. There was but one man, besides his secretary, with whom he sometimes exchanged a word—Mr. Rhyl Owen—who went for him, under promises of strictest secrecy, to a certain lawyer at monthly periods for money. He spent every evening of his self-tormenting life, and almost the whole day, absolutely alone; and he chose for his retreat a shabby genteel second floor in the heart of London. Why?

And yet he was not unhappy. The sturdy
health he enjoyed, the clearness of his eye, the
steadiness of his nerves, the coldness of his manner, showed that he was happy in his own way.
Why had he left the world? He was no self-
starving ascetic; that was clear from the appearance of a kitchener complete in all its parts,
with a bright array of stewpans, pots, and culi-
nary apparatus, for which his servant, a woman,
brought him every morning, before he was up,
and set out in readiness for him, a basket with
the day's provisions. In the evening she came
again, and put his dishes in the cupboard
out of his sight for him. His bookshelves contained half a dozen works on cookery; the rest
were all French novels, chiefly new ones; and
with these and the periodicals, the Hermit found
enough to read. His day was uniform, and
perhaps monotonous: he took breakfast at ten;
at twelve his secretary worked with him till half-
past two or three; till six or so he was busy
preparing his own dinner, to which he devoted
his whole mind. After eating it and taking a
glass or two of claret, his evening was free for
reading. He was, it will be seen, a recluse of

quite a different stamp from those of history. Nor was he without other amusements. A chess table stood in the window, on which he would work out problems and send them to papers. He had a piano, on which he discoursed with sufficient skill, but without pretensions to artistic cultivation, and he amused himself sometimes with making water-colour sketches. The subjects of these—as Dicky knew, having often seen them on the table— were all variations of a single theme. They represented military life in various phases. There were the awkward squad, the church parade, the regimental steeplechase, the garrison ball, the mess-room, the billiard table; and there was besides a picture which Mr. Lilliecrip painted again and again. The treatment varied and the figures, but the background was always the same—cold, snow, and ice; a handful of men, sometimes one man alone, wrapped in great coats and armed, creeping warily to trench work; among them always one tall and handsome young man, in whom Dicky recognized his employer, the mysterious Hermit of Lowland-street.

A battle-piece hung upon the wall; over the mantelshelf was a sword; these were further proofs that the solitary had been in the army. Why, then, had he taken a hatred to the world and left it?

Perhaps he did not hate it: the papers and periodicals proved that he took an interest in what went on. The latest *Army List* on the table showed that he followed the promotion of his old officers; and what was the meaning of those piles of manuscript which he was perpetually reading, dictating, and correcting? And yet he hid himself, so jealously hid himself that high and close wire blinds were adjusted to the windows to prevent his face being visible to the street or the opposite houses. He appeared to deny himself in nothing. A box of cigars, of a choice brand, stood on his sideboard; a row of pipes were in the rack; with them a jar, the end of whose being—the holding of tobacco—was accomplished, and the room had a fine and constant perfume of smoking. There was a spirit case; and once, the door of the sideboard having been left open, Dicky caught sight of a pile of bottles, some of them with silver tops.

"Champagne!" he murmured, with bated breath. It was a drink which he often dreamed of, but had never tasted, even in its humbler forms. And if the man was so rich as to afford all these luxuries, why did he live in Lowland-street? Why did he live alone? And why, Dicky thought with indignation and sorrow, why did he give a paltry fifteen shillings a week to his secretary?

"I was at William the Fourth — yes — ascended the throne 1830, and died 1837. Of course. Are you ready?"

"Quite ready, sir."

"The first time I saw the Duke of Clarence was in the year 1818, when I was myself a child of eight. I was in the Park with my mother, an old friend and sincere well-wisher of the royal and gallant sailor. He took me in his arms on being told who I was; pressing me to his breast, his royal highness, who was remarkably fond of children, said: 'A damned fine child—a monstrous great boy—a chip of the old block. I congratulate you, Lady ——, on your son.' As he put me down I felt a tear fall upon my cheek—one of the few that William

the Fourth was ever known to shed. I did not
know then that my father and he had been
fellow-midshipmen many years before. The
Duke of Clarence never forgot an old com-
rade."

Dicky wrote down this interesting and illus-
trative anecdote with a sense of greatness being
thrust upon him. He was in the presence of a
man who had been in the arms of royalty. He
instinctively gathered up his feet under the
chair, so as to hide the state of his heels, which
were really not fit for the companion of kings to
see, and listened for more.

"The next time was in the year '36. His
Majesty was pleased to send for me, being
informed that I was in the neighbourhood of
Windsor. I found him on the slopes, and he
conversed with me for half an hour, chiefly on
questions connected with the state of the army,
a subject in which he was supposed to take little
interest. Opposed as I was to his Majesty's
rigid conservatism, I felt myself obliged to ask
permission to state my views at length. This
he granted, and dismissed me, after hearing
them, with every mark of gracious condescen-

sion. I feel bound to say that on this, as on every other occasion, I found William the Fourth most affable, clear-headed, and intelligent; and I bear witness the more readily to this effect, because detractors have sneered at his Majesty's abilities: these were, in reality, of no common order. I had at one time the idea of writing a political history of the reign of William the Fourth, but was deterred by the private nature of much of the information which I should have used.

" History is based upon lies, and it is impossible to get at the truth. That is only known to the diplomatist, who never talks: it dies with him. When I was in Vienna, Metternich confessed to me the whole secret history of the campaign of 1815, which I shall write as soon as I find time. Who would have guessed that Waterloo was a put-up thing?

"Wellington I knew well. He was very fond of entertaining me, during long evening talks, with stories about Napoleon's generals. His opinion of them greatly varied. Marmont, he said, was a devil of a fellow. Massena kept him awake at night. Soult never made him forget to say his prayers for a week. 'Gad!' he used to say, 'even you would have had your work cut out with Soult.' He thought a great deal more perhaps than I really deserved of my personal courage and military genius. It was generous of him.

"Talleyrand was excessively fond of boiled pork, broad beans, and pease pudding. He told me once, dining at the Austrian Embassy, that he could have wished to be an Englishman, in order to enjoy the oftener what he considered our national food. It is not generally known that he ordered it to be served every day when beans were in season.

"Sir Robert Peel, Lord George Bentinck, Bulwer Lytton, Lord Melbourne, and I, were once taking supper after a late debate. After midnight, we set ourselves to foretelling the future, a thing which the military diplomatist alone can do with certainty. It is now thirty years ago, and I remember, though I do not boast of it, that I foretold exactly the war between Germany and France, being only out a trifle in the year: I placed that too soon. Bentinck, who was really a man of the highest genius, prophesied that very same evening the escape of the prisoner of Ham and the beginning of the end for Louis Philippe. Could Ezekiel himself have done more?

"When these men died, England had no great men left. The legislators and diplomatists of the present day are pigmies in comparison with the school to which they belonged. The great art of the diplomatist, according to their traditions, was to know the exact moment to *invent* —to invent with freedom and facility, and to invent with a truthful face. I have often heard poor Lord George declare that an evening with Austrian and French diplomatists was like a short campaign; everything depended upon the accurate gauge of your adversary's truth.—Have you taken that down correctly, Mr. Carew?"

"All down, sir—'gauge of truth.'"

"Good—another sheet. 'Recollections of Lord Melbourne.'"

Dicky obeyed, and—his thoughts wandering —proceeded to write without catching the meaning of the words. The drama in his mind meanwhile was going on. "Spare me, Carew—spare me! You have the secret of my life; you have

7—2

in your power the honour of a house; you can blight a noble name. Be merciful as you are strong."

This was the masterpiece of Dick's imagination, and a part of the duologue with which he amused his weary occupation. He was writing something quite different, but no doubt it was almost as great nonsense.

"There was a time, old man, when you spurned the humble amanuensis. He came up thirsty; you had champagne in the cupboard, and there was a refreshing tap at the nearest corner, but you offered him neither ale nor wine. His boots were down at heel, and you had not the humane generosity to present him with a new pair; he was hard up, and you knew it, and never raised his pay. Old man, I'll have my bond!"

"— A cry was heard, which reached from St. James's Palace to the lonely smoking-room of the club where the disappointed peer sat brooding: 'Long live our youthful Queen!' He sprang to his feet and uttered a cry of gratitude.—Is that down? Take care; these are among the most precious of my recollections."

He spoke in a slow and deliberate manner throughout, so that his secretary might easily follow.

"I was reading over what you wrote yesterday, and I find that your inadvertence allowed me to make a statement which is ridiculous. You actually permitted me—you, my private secretary—to state that Beau Brummell, Count d'Orsay, and Prince Albert were my guests on the same day at the Star and Garter."

"You said so, sir."

"Nonsense. How could I say so? If it was not true, how could I say so? Take care, Mr. Carew, take care. I am afraid you do not pay proper attention to accuracy. Had I not detected that mistake my enemies would have certainly accused me of inaccuracy, and perhaps the very authenticity of my recollections would have been impugned. I looked for better things, Mr. Carew."

Dicky saw his anticipations of a rise in salary vanish and become the shadow of a hope. It was hard on him, because he was afraid of interrupting Mr. Lilliecrip in the full flow of reminiscence, and he certainly had described a

banquet in which, he being the host, the late
Prince Consort, Beau Brummell, Count d'Orsay,
and other distinguished personages had figured
as his guests.

"Would you like me, sir, to take the memoirs
away with me, and revise them by the help of
the *Annual Register?*"

"Certainly not, sir. You will understand that
you have no right to breathe a word as to these
memoirs. Should you do so, remember *that I
shall hear of it.* You will then lose, not only
your present employment, but any future honorarium which I may think of bestowing upon
you."

This Hermit, it will have been perceived, was
engaged in the preparation of Personal Reminiscences. In order to avoid the raising of
expectations doomed to be disappointed, it
may be mentioned at once that his personal
reminiscences were a series—an immense long
series—of personal lies, figments, and imagina-
tions, of which the world had never seen the
like. He had not been in contact with any of
the great men whose names he used so freely;
he had never spoken to one of them; but he

wanted to do something that would live after him, and he was gratifying the vanity of a morbid mind by compiling a gigantic work of pretended memoirs. He proposed to bequeath these to the British Museum, with an injunction that the packet was not to be opened for seventy-five years. The man was preparing a lie, which with its dullness, heaviness, and stupidity was likely to weigh heavily on posterity, unless these very qualities caused the imposture to be detected.

Mr. Lilliecrip sat down again, and passed his white hand across his forehead.

"I am fatigued to-day, I think. My memory is sluggish. Tell me, Mr. Carew, without mentioning names—the world is nothing more to me, and I care not to hear its names—what people think of me, or what that small part of London in which you move thinks. What is said about me?"

Here was an astonishing thing for the Hermit to ask. For more than three years Dicky had worked with him, and had never exchanged a word save on necessary subjects.

"What do they say? Do they talk about me?"

Dicky remembered that the conversation, only the night before, had turned exclusively upon the Hermit: had he been of an entirely truthful nature, which unhappily was not the case, he would have repeated for Mr. Lilliecrip's information the speech he made on the occasion. It was as follows: he delivered it with much freedom of utterance, being then in the first stage only of intoxication, standing before the fire, and waving a pipe in his right hand :—

"Gentlemen, with regard to my esteemed friend, whom you call the Hermit of Lowland-street, I am not, as many of you are aware, allowed to reveal the important secrets which my mysterious employer has been good enough to intrust to my care. He is, however, as you may imagine, no mystery to me. Is he rich? is he nobly born? is he generous? is he princely in his disposition? I say nothing. I answer neither Yes nor No. What is the reason for his strange retirement? Gentlemen, I must not tell you. It was only this morning, in the splendidly furnished suite of chambers, externally humble, where we transact our business—

chambers in which everything is as magnificently appointed as in Windsor Castle, or in my noble friend's ancestral halls—"

"He is a swell, then," said a listener. "By Jove, he must have done something *very* bad."

"It was only this morning he said to me, 'Carew, if there were any other man in the world to whom I could confide my history, I would not give you this trouble. I feel that you are my only true friend, and I fear I inflict too much upon you.' He had the goodness to say that—"

"Wouldn't it be better, Dicky, if he were to ask you for the measure of your feet, and buy you a new pair of boots?"

Dicky took no notice of this personal allusion to his poverty.

"He went on to say that what he offered me now was nothing, simply nothing, compared with what he was going to give when— But I am speaking too freely. As for the ridiculous honorarium which—pah! gentlemen, I blow it away like this cloud."

Later on in the evening, Dicky, growing truthful under the influence of gin-and-water, wept as he confessed, amid the smiles of his friends, the mean and curmudgeon-like spirit of the Hermit, and the degrading task of writing from dictation which was his daily lot. It was curious that at no stage of intoxication would he confess the nature of his employer's papers.

However, Dicky did not, in answer to the question of his master, think fit to communicate the substance of his speech.

"They *do* talk, I suppose," said Mr. Lilliecrip. "It is not a usual thing for a man to immure himself in four dingy walls, and deny himself society, is it?"

"They talk, sir: they will talk, you know—even quite common people."

Dicky was a little embarrassed.

"What do they say, then?"

"Well, really, sir, wild talk, mostly. It would offend you, perhaps."

"Offend me? Do you really suppose— Come, Mr. Carew, what do people say of me?"

"They don't know what to say about you. Some think you are the rightful Sir Roger Tichborne in hiding for something done in the Bush."

"Good. Go on."

"Some say you are the real heir to a crown, and paid to keep yourself out of the way."

"That is better."

"Most believe that you are a murderer in hiding, and there's more than one has given information of you to the police, in hope of getting a reward. I have heard of people consulting old newspapers of fourteen years ago to find out who was watched by the police then, and they have stood me drinks, sir—dozens of drinks —in order to find out any little hint that may help them."

"This is interesting," said the Hermit. "A cheap way of getting popularity and notoriety, too."

"They call you the Hermit of Lowland-street, and there's a man connected with the *Daily Firework* wants to make an article out of you."

"Tell him he'd better not," said the Recluse. "Tell him, if he does, I'll find out all about him —his debts and his sins, his weak places and his discreditable doings—and I'll ruin him. Tell him that."

He actually impressed Dicky with so deep a

sense of a power in reserve, that he accepted this threat as quite within his reach, and went on—

"Some think you must have forged a will, and are living on the proceeds; or else that you are a—"

"Bah!" said the Solitary. "It is stupid. What does it matter what they say? About yourself now, Mr. Carew?"

Dicky's heart beat. Here, then, was the long-looked-for opportunity. Now for the increase of salary.

"I was about to venture, sir, to speak of myself. Three years is a good spell at fifteen shillings a week—"

"You were about to say that you were sorry the work was not worth more than half; and you would have been right, Mr. Carew, quite right."

This was a damper.

"What *I* was about to say was, that your appearance is discreditable, and that I shall advance you the money to purchase a new suit, to be stopped out of your pay at the rate of five shillings a week. That is all, Mr. Carew."

He placed a packet with money in his hands, and nodded dismissal.

"Stay—stay; there was another thing. I hear now and then a pleasing voice singing in the room below me to the piano. I am absolutely careless about the world, but you may tell me anything you know about the voice. No, sir— no gush; no names. I want nothing about the history of these people—quite commonplace and vulgar people, in a commonplace and vulgar street. Answer me without unnecessary words. Rich or poor?"

"Poor. Were rich."

"Is the owner of the voice young and pretty, or old and—"

"Young and pretty. Twenty."

"How many in family?"

"Two sisters. Ladies. Unmarried. One is an artist."

"That will do, Mr. Carew—that will do. To-morrow, if you please, be more punctual. Remember what I say, that if in your drinking bouts—I know your habits, sir—you let out what you do here, you will repent it in such sober earnest as you little dream of."

Dicky retired humbly. With regard to the money, his first thought was naturally to spend it in a wild and rollicking carouse; but better thoughts prevailed. How if Mr. Lilliecrip found him out? How if, in the blindness of his wrath, he should carry into execution his threats, and make *him* repent?

"To be sure," Dicky reflected, taking comfort, "I am a soft-hearted man, and I repent very easily."

"Strange," said the Hermit, "how that voice haunts me. For the first time these fourteen years I want to see another face. What is coming over me?"

As he spoke, the voice began again to a simple accompaniment of the piano, singing a simple ballad to an ancient tune. It was Adie, taking one of the few pleasures left to her, to sing and play while Marion painted.

He stood still and listened. Presently it ceased, and he caught the low ripple of girlish laughter, and the voices of girls talking. His heart beat and his knees trembled.

"I am a fool," he said. "I am fooled by that idiot, Carew. He takes some vulgar little milliner animal for a lady, and a rosy cheek for beauty."

He spent the rest of the day over his dinner.

In the evening his man of business, Mr. Owen, knocked at his door. Mr. Lilliecrip was sitting by the fire in the soft light of a moderator lamp. He was in evening dress: this Hermit, had he donned the friar's serge and lived in those miserable quarters on the river Coquet whereof the ballad sings, would have made it a rule to change the simple gown and the rope for black coat and white tie in the evening. He was playing with a cup of coffee, and lazily thinking of taking a pipe over the latest novel. On the entrance of the schoolmaster he finished the coffee.

"Pray excuse me a moment, Mr. Owen," he said, with great politeness, "and take a chair."

Mr. Owen placed a chair in the middle of the room, and sat himself down, with his feet under it, in such a position that he could not be accused of curiously prying into anything while the owner was not in the room. Mr. Lilliecrip, however, returned immediately, wearing a velvet jacket and a smoking cap.

"Always change your evening coat, Mr. Owen, before smoking; the tobacco *will* linger about the cloth."

Mr. Owen grunted. The advice is superfluous to a man who has but one coat.

"I have been for the money as usual," he said. "Here it is—thirty-three, five, seven. Count it."

The Solitary counted it, and dropped it in his pocket.

"Messrs. Crackett and Charges want to see you. They say there is an opportunity for advancing your interests."

"I told them to send no messages, and to write me no letters. I will not be worried with investments."

"That's all, then," said Mr. Owen, rising abruptly.

"One moment, Owen — your advice, if you please. There's a girl downstairs."

"Two," said the schoolmaster—"three, in fact, counting my Winifred, and I don't see why she shouldn't be counted."

"Nor I, I am sure. Count her, by all means. One of the three is pretty, I am told—not that I care, of course; not that it matters to me."

"They are all three pretty, and as good as gold."

"There is one that sings."

"They all three sing. What is that to you?"

Mr. Rhyl Owen was gruff of speech with Mr. Lilliecrip, the result of fourteen years' occasional communication with that gentleman.

"If he's not polite with you, he'll bully you," said Mr. Owen, thinking about him. "He is a cur that licks your hand one minute and bites it the next."

"What are the girls to you, Mr. Lilliecrip?"

"I am sometimes a little lonely. Do you think that one of them—they are all, I suppose, poor—would like to come up here, and sit with me, read with me, talk to me in the evening?"

"No, she would not. None of them would," the schoolmaster replied, with great decision.

"I would pay her, you know."

"Mr. Lilliecrip, two of them are ladies, and the other earns her bread in a better way than talking to old fools."

"You are rude to-night. Am I not fit company for them, do you mean?"

Mr. Owen was silent.

" Come, sir, tell me what you do mean."

" I mean, Mr. Lilliecrip, that neither of the young ladies shall come up here if I can prevent it. They are real ladies, born and bred. As for that, my Winifred should not come here either."

" Well, well, Owen, I cannot afford to quarrel with you, or else I should have to find some one else to go out for me. Perhaps you are right; people might talk if a young lady came to my rooms alone, though I am surely grey enough and old enough."

" Old enough, certainly," said Mr. Owen, drily. The young lady's brother lives in the house, too. You had better speak to him about it."

" Ah!" Mr. Lilliecrip changed colour, but very slightly; " is he—is he a gentleman, too? Lowland-street seems to be suffering from an invasion of ladies and gentlemen."

" Oh, yes—he's a gentleman, and a fire-eater too. Lord, Mr. Lilliecrip, put it out of your thoughts. Why, he'd murder you, that young gentleman would, so fierce as he is, if he'd even the thought of his sister visiting you in this room. We must first know who and what you

are, Mr. Lilliecrip, and why you have shut yourself up."

"And a pretty girl?"

"They are both beautiful girls; and one is a
lovely creature. God bless her!" said Mr. Owen,
getting up to go.

When Mr. Lilliecrip was left alone, he began
to ponder over his cigar. After fourteen years
of solitude, the thought of a beautiful girl being
in the same house, the possibility that she might
enliven his room by her presence, agitated him.
How should he get to know this beautiful girl?

"It is strange," he said; "I cannot understand. Fourteen years of peace and content,
and to-night—all from a voice and a few words;
one would think I was only beginning the
prison. Could it be possible for me to leave
the place and go out again?" He rose, and
walked up and down the room, his face working
with the emotion of some disturbing memory.
"No, never!" he cried; "never! I will stay
here till I die!"

CHAPTER V.

THE April mornings are sunlit at six, even in the heart of London, and there is a fine painting light for those who are able to get up for it. The early morning was Marion's time of peace and quiet labour; she would be alone. How great a blessing it is to be alone for an hour or two in the day can only, I suppose, be appreciated by women who live together. It is one of the many evils of poverty that the poor have no solitude possible. As the social ladder descends, the necessity of a life in common becomes more marked. The suburban villa has its three sitting-rooms for a family of half a dozen; but the ladies of the "lower middle class" have to sleep, eat, read, work, and play in the same room.

In the early morning, when the air is clear
and bright, Marion took fresh courage, and
clothed herself with new faith and hope. Above
all, she worked: that soul is never quite unhappy which can take a healthy pleasure in
work for its own sake. Marion was, for the
first time, after four years of copying, engaged
upon an original picture. She was ambitious, as
most young painters are. She did not yet fully
understand that a work of art must be a copy of
Nature itself, and not a reminiscence or a reflec-
tion; and her picture had the fault of being
drawn from the inspiration of other masters.
There are plenty of such pictures in every Royal
Academy — you find a familiar touch here, and
another there; you are reminded of one master
here, and another there. Nature is at second
hand — the light hardly fits the season; the
flowers do not fit with each other; the primrose
and the nightshade are painted blossoming side
by side; and yet, for some subtle grace and
secret charm of their own, the pictures are
bought and loved. It was so with Marion. She
had chosen an Italian subject, who had never
been in Italy; she had put in Italian flowers,

who knew not an Italian summer; country figures, who had never seen a *contadina;* an Italian sky, who had never been out of England; a dress which was never worn under the canopy of heaven; a light which never shone on earth or ocean; and yet, for one redeeming touch it had, the picture was warm with life and feeling. She had taken a scene from Browning's "Pippa passes," a poem which — if its author had only for once been able to wed melodious verse to the sweetest poetical thought; if he had only tried, just for once, to write lines which should not make the cheeks of those that read them to ache, the front teeth of those who declaim them to splinter and fly, the ears of those that hear them to crack—would have been a thing to rest himself upon for ever, and receive the applause of the world. To the gods it seemed otherwise. Browning, who might have led us like Hamelin the piper, has chosen the worse part. He will be so deeply wise that he cannot express his thought; he will be so full of profundities that he requires a million of lines to express them in; he will leave music and melody to Swinburne; he will leave grace and sweetness to Tennyson; and in fifty years' time, who will read Browning? Let us return to our sheep.

Marion had chosen the place where Pippa passes singing:—

> " The year's at the spring,
>   The day's at the morn,
>   Morning's at seven,
>   The hill-side's dew pearled;
>   The lark's on the wing,
>   The snail's on the thorn,
>   God's in His Heaven,
>   All's right with the world."

Oh, strong poet of the densest tympanum, to write those third and fourth lines—

> " The hill-side's dew pearled!"

Was there ever such a stuttering collocation of syllables to confound the reader and utterly destroy a sweet little lyric?

Pippa was Adrienne, Marion's model. She was passing in the bright early morning, singing as she went, unconscious of her words, and dangling her grapes before her; a figure full of health, youth, and beauty; Adrienne with the least possible darkening of the eyebrows and

the hair; not an Italian face at all; sweet-lipped
Adie, tall, delicate, graceful—not a silk-weaver,
not Pippa, not a workwoman, not the heroine
of Browning's noble dream; an English girl, in
a bright clear sunshine, with strong shadows,
which lay black under the vine-leaves and
behind the stones, and set off her sweetness as
a crystal mounted in an ebony setting; and
behind the unconscious girl a face and the back
of a head—the face of a man who catches the
words. They strike his ear with a force the
girl knows nothing of; the glamour of a devilish
passion falls from him, and he sees the awful
thing—too late—in its true light. In the head of
the woman that looks to him you may, if you
can, imagine the wonder that is in her unseen
face, and the horror of the awaking. Pippa
sings her song and passes—

> "God's in His Heaven,
>   All's right with the world."

The picture was nearly finished; the principal
figure—a half figure—was completed; the heads
were worked up; only the flowers and acces-
sories were as yet to be filled in.

Marion worked contentedly from half-past

five to eight at her canvas. She was not unhappy, provided there was money to give her
two children enough to eat: it was all she
worked for now. If she dreamed of anything
better, it seemed a long way off. She was their
natural protector: to her they were the two
children always, helpless, not quite to be
trusted; a little perverse—at least, one of them
—but always lovable, always to be treated with
a fond consideration. At eight Adie appeared,
and began to make the breakfast. This was the
happiest time that the girls had. In the evening
there was always the drop of bitterness in the
cup, the discontent of comparison, the absence
of their brother. In the morning they were
alone, for Fred seldom rose till nine or ten,
and they could talk. Presently Marion, keeping
silence on the doctor's proposals, began to talk,
as usual, of money matters.

" Five shillings, Adie, dear," she said, giving
her that amount. "It is not a great deal for a
long day's work copying, is it? But it is as much
as Mr. Burls would give me. After all, I dare
say it is more than one deserves. Why do they
always pay women so much worse than men?"

"Because they are not strong enough to knock the cheats down and beat them, as men would do," said Adie, vindictively.

She took the money, and dropped it into her purse, where Dr. Chacomb's five pounds were lying: the accusing jingle of the coins reminded her unpleasantly of her promise, and struck her soul with a note of remorse. It was as if she had sold herself to deceive her sister.

"It is enough, at any rate," she said, "for to-day. You shall have some dinner when you come home, dear. Not a dinner-tea; you shall have some steak, and I will get you a pint of claret, if—if—oh, if Fred does not want it all. You want a little wine so badly, dear."

"Let Fred have two shillings, Adie, and I will do without the claret. Besides, it is ridiculous for us to talk about wine, with our fortunes at this low ebb."

"Marion, you are looking pale. Do not work so hard; things will get right somehow—I am sure they will. Fred says he has always felt certain they will."

Marion shook her head. She was not hopeful this morning; perhaps because the sky had clouded over since she left off work for breakfast.

"Fred will get a situation," Adie went on, trying to talk cheerfully, and working the talk round, somehow, to a point. "That is, if he gets friends to back him up. The poor boy wants friends badly, if only to keep him out of the billiard-rooms. Perhaps I shall be able to get something to do; but it seems as if I can do nothing at all. I might teach French, it is true, if anybody would believe that I knew it. Marion, let us talk it together every day, for fear of my forgetting my only accomplishment. I cannot play well enough to teach music, and I know nothing else—nothing. My dear, I am horribly helpless and selfish. I let you work day after day for us, and never seem to do anything."

"Adie," Marion patted her cheek, "I do not want you to do anything."

Adie sighed.

"Marion," she whispered, laying her arm on her sister's neck, "Marion, tell me, if you saw a way—if any one told you of a way, would you not like to escape out of all this dreadful misery

and poverty? Think of yesterday, and our
starving. Think of my having to go and beg
Mr. Owen to give me something to eat. And
Fred coming home at night smoking an expen-
sive cigar, with no money left of all he took
from you the day before. Oh, the shame of it!"

There were times when Adie's view of Fred's
conduct was harsher than Marion's.

"Let us face the present," said Marion, conscious of what her sister meant. "See, dear, I
shall take the pictures to Mr. Hermann. He
always buys what I bring him, though he does
not give much. Mr. Burls said that if he had
any money he would have given four guineas a
head. Mr. Hermann ought at least to give me a
guinea each—that makes five guineas, and then
we will have a little claret to do us both good."

It seemed a very small matter to Adie—this
chance of five guineas—in the face of all the
possibilities opened up by the doctor.

"But, Marion, suppose a way were to lie open
unto us? Suppose—O, Marion, you who work
so hard for us all, what if we could get back to
something like the old life again, and be at
rest?"

Marion looked at her inquiringly. She knew, by a sudden intuition, and by the flushed cheeks and drooping eyelashes, that her sister had been talking to the doctor, and about herself.

"If the way were not impossible, Adie."

"Oh, what could be impossible? Marion, dear, you know what I am thinking of. It seems such a simple thing. And think what it means for you and me and Fred. Only try to think. Servants to wait upon us again; ladies and gentlemen to talk to; dress—proper dress—to wear; money to spend. Oh, Marion, how can you say it is impossible? It would not be to me."

Marion heard her sister with a heavy heart.

"What did Dr. Chacomb say to you?"

"He told me he loved you; and he asked me to speak to you myself. I promised I would, Marion; was I wrong?"

Marion caressed the fair cheek that looked up to her.

"Don't talk to him again about it, my dear. Try to realise only that it is impossible, and that we must face the present. Have patience and a little hope."

"Sometimes I have hope. Sometimes I think Fred is right, and we shall all three go back to take our proper place like disinherited princes and princesses; and sometimes, Marion—it is too selfish, when you do everything for us—sometimes I think you might do more. Don't say it is impossible, dear. I have been lying awake half the night thinking it all over."

"My poor child," said Marion, taking Adie's face in her hands, "my poor child! it is so hard that you should be unhappy."

"And you, dear; is it not hard for you too? Is it quite impossible, Marion? See, dear"—she spoke hurriedly, as if the subject was too much for her—"see, dear, here we starve and are miserable; with *him* we should at least be warm and comfortable, and have no anxiety—think of that. Think of waking up every morning without feeling that there will be no dinner the next day unless we work for it; think of not having to find money for Fred's extravagances; think of being able to wear decent things; think of the change we should have in our lives. He is kind, Marion; I am sure he is kind. To be sure, he is not very young; but what of that? He does not want your love, he says; he only wants you to marry him, and then he will try to get your love afterwards."

"My dear, could I marry any one unless I loved him first?"

"Why not? I would. If Dr. Chacomb had come to me instead of to you, and asked me to marry him, I should have jumped for joy. Love! What is all the nonsense people talk about love? I cannot understand it. I want to be well dressed and rich—that is the real happiness."

"You will know better later, Adie. Do not let us talk about it any more. Dr. Chacomb knows that it can never be. I told him so last night. I think he is kind, too; but it is impossible, Adie. Do not say anything more about it. Put it quite out of your thoughts, and let us try to make the best of the little we have."

"But we have nothing," said Adie, with her musical laugh, "nothing at all. Marion, I have often read about the duty of being contented with little; but not even the books which are the hardest about duty, and make it the most difficult to get to Heaven, ever say anything about the duty of being contented with nothing. Be reasonable, dear Marion, and discontented."

It was after breakfast that this conversation took place. The girls always took their breakfast first, the head of the family appearing later.

As Adie finished her philosophical remarks, Fred appeared, fully equipped for his journey "into the City." His way there might have seemed, to any who saw him start, a circuitous route, for on reaching Oxford-street he invariably turned west. It does not do, however, to be always guided by appearances. He may have "fetched a compass," like St. Paul, and worked round by way of Battersea. His equanimity, disturbed by the doctor the evening before, was completely restored. After all, he was—and he knew it well enough—an idle rascal. He never had done anything, and he hoped to pass wholly through life without doing anything. Besides, Fred's anger was like a fire of chips—it exhausted itself, and was quickly spent. Storms in shallow lakes quickly subside. This morning he was fresh, and even radiant.

Marion's artistic instincts furnished, perhaps, one of the reasons why she never grew tired of this idle and good-for-nothing brother. She loved him for his beauty and his grace. It was always a pleasure for her eyes to rest upon the lines of his form. His face, which to a man seemed wanting in depth, was to her as full of depth and possible emotion as the illimitable sea. She made perpetual excuse for him; she cheerfully gave him all she could; she made him her type of that divine beauty which, man or woman, the best of us dream of and long after. Her face lit up when he entered the room and kissed her in his lordly, off-hand way.

"A lovely morning, Marion. Are you going far? Adie, sew a button on my glove for me, please. Will you come for a walk this afternoon? I can be back at two o'clock for you."

He went to the window, and looked out. A cloud crossed his face.

"Marion, I think that, considering the state of our finances and how unlucky we have been of late, it is hardly a time for charity."

"What do you mean, Fred?"

Marion was getting together her portfolio.

"I mean that the woman I have seen you talking to once or twice is hanging about in the

street, intending no doubt to waylay you directly
you leave the place. Now, Marion, please remember charity begins at home. We cannot
well afford out-door relief just now. No doubt
it is extremely creditable and respectable to
have a pensioner—even such a disreputable pensioner as that."

Marion's hands shook a little; but she steadied
herself.

"I dare say she will not want any money, Fred.
Now I am ready. Give me good luck, Adie,
dear."

Fred watched her from the window.

"There are the usual children hanging about
her skirts," he said, impatiently. "Really, I think
Marion considers herself a mother in Israel. If
there is a child in trouble, or a woman in distress,
Marion must be consulted. Why cannot we live
unknown, and not talked about? I fully expect
Marion will be reported in a daily paper for a
philanthropist."

Presently he saw the woman he had noticed
cross the street.

"I thought so," he said, impatiently. "Upon
my word, you know, Adie, it's too ridiculous.

Here we are, almost starving, and Marion throwing the money away upon street beggars! She has crossed over—I knew she would—and is begging of Marion. Now they are talking at the corner. Now they have gone off together. Who *is* the woman, Adie?"

"I don't know. I asked once, but was told not to ask any more—some poor woman who knows Marion."

"I shall make it my business," said Fred, pompously, "to inquire. I am the head of the family, and I will not have secrets kept from me."

"Don't be a goose, Fred. You are no more the head of the family than I am. As if anything you could say, or I either, would turn Marion an inch from her own path. Poor Marion!"

"I wish I could see the way to persuade her to make money," said her brother. "Look at this canvas—she spends half her time over a thing like that!" It was her unfinished painting. "What will she do with it? Who will buy it? And when I proposed to her to make a steady income by giving lessons, she refused. Just the same the other day, when I saw an advertisement that would have suited me admirably: 'A gentleman by birth and education wanted to advance about twelve hundred pounds in a sleeping partnership'—sleeping, Adie—'from which he will draw at least a hundred per cent. by way of profits." Think of it, you know— nothing to do but to draw twelve hundred a year or so! I showed it to Marion, and asked her to sell out her little fortune and lend it to me. She refused. She said nothing would induce her to part with the money, not even to make my fortune with it."

"Yes, Marion told me about it. You see, Fred, if you had lost the money—which you most likely would have done—where should we be? Now, if everything else fails, we always have the fifty pounds a year to fall back upon."

"Just like women," Fred growled; "they never understand the simplest rules of investment. I could make that miserable fifty into five thousand if I had it!"

"O, Fred, you will never make your own fortune or ours either, poor boy! Sit down and have your tea."

He complied with the invitation. Adie sat opposite, and talked.

"Such a chance, Fred, too, as Marion has missed. Oh, such a chance! We shall never have another like it—never!"

"What chance, Adie?"

His face flushed, as hers had done, at the mere thought of being rich.

"Fred," she put on her most solemn tones, "a rich man wants to marry Marion!"

"A rich man?"

"And to provide for you, and to take care of me. But she has refused him—twice."

"Who is it?"

"It is Dr. Chacomb."

"I would rather she married the Devil!" he said, hotly.

"Don't swear, Fred."

"I would. Do you know that he has insulted me—that he insulted me last night even? He called me—well, never mind! Marion shall never have my permission to marry Dr. Chacomb."

"You *are* a goose, Fred; you really are. You cannot really think that either of us is going to ask your permission to do anything we want to do. Be sensible, if you can. Play at being the head of the family, as you call it, outside, where perhaps they don't know that Marion works for all and provides for all—poor Marion!"

"Are you too going to turn against me, Adie?" he asked.

"No, Fred. I shall never turn against you. You are like me. We are both of us the same; and you are my very own brother. You *can't* help yourself, my poor boy, any more than I can. And if anything happened to Marion— Well, let me tell you about it, without any more heroics! Dr. Chacomb is a very kind-hearted man. I should live with him and Marion. We should have a carriage, and a box at the Opera, and—"

"Dreams, Adie! The man has no money. He lives on what he can borrow from his cousin!"

"But he *has* money, I tell you. He is rich. He is a successful physician, and the founder of the Royal Hospital for Gout. Why, he makes five thousand pounds a year, he tells me.

O, Fred, what a brother-in-law, if Marion would only see it!"

Fred became thoughtful.

"Does he do all that? I know how to find out. There's a chemist fellow comes to our billiard-rooms—not a gentleman, you know—who knows all about doctors and that class of people"—Fred always spoke of persons who earned their livelihood as "that class of people." "Now I think of it, Chacomb did have a respectable appearance last night when he came here. I don't like him, Adie. Hang it! you can't like a man who calls you an idle— Well, but if he *has* this large income, and if he will take care of you and look after me, I shall not let any prejudice of mine stand in the way. I withdraw my opposition, Adie."

"That's very good of you, Fred," Adie laughed.

"I do not forget," the young man went on, "the house to which I belong, whose head I am. It has always been usual for the representative of the name to have a voice in the alliances contracted by the members of the family."

"That's very grand, my dear brother; and it

is a great blessing to feel that we have a head with a proper sense of dignity. If you had arms as well— No, Fred, I won't tease. But Marion won't have him."

"Adie, suppose—I only say suppose—the doctor were to shift his proposal to the younger sister. What would you say?"

The girl reddened.

"I told Marion that I should jump for joy. But I don't think I should. I like Dr. Chacomb very much—I do, indeed; but I don't think I could marry him when it came actually to the point. However, that is not to the point. I am quite sure that he will not ask me, and I am also quite sure that he is as rich as he says he is. Besides, Fred, if poor Gerald never comes home again, he is the heir to Chacomb."

Fred whistled.

"So he is, so he is. Adie, we must try and bring it off if we can. My dear child, fancy going back to Comb Leigh, the masters of Chacomb!"

"Oh, the delight! Fred, fancy sitting by the dear old beach and hearing the waves beat against the rocks again! Oh, think of the cliff, and the garden, and the flowers. You and I would live in the rosary; we would walk about as we used to do, and lie on the grass and eat strawberries, and have piles—piles of roses in the drawing-room every day, and all the new music. I should wear white all the summer."

"And in the season we would come to town," said her brother, flushing with enthusiasm.

"Yes; and you would give me a pony carriage, wouldn't you?" Then she burst into a laugh that ended in a sob. "But it's no good. We are here—*nous voici plantés*—in Lowland-street. Marion will not have him, and we grow poorer every day."

Their faces dropped, and the sunlight of imagination disappeared behind a cloud.

Quoth Fred, after a little pause—

"Have you got any money, Adie?"

"Marion gave me five shillings, and—and—Fred, don't be angry, but Dr. Chacomb offered me five pounds when he heard that we had no money—all in gold—and I took them. Here they are."

She spread out the sovereigns, with Marion's

poor five shillings, on the table, and looked up
at her brother in a little doubt.

He knitted his brows with the gravity of
Epictetus the moralist.

"That was wrong, child. That was very
wrong. Women never seem to have the same
sense of honour as men. You ought not to have
taken the money. Remember that men never
take money of each other, unless they win it at
billiards, cards, or betting. Then, of course, it
is a different thing. I could not myself, for instance, poor as we are, accept money of any one
—even offered me by my best friend."

This was very noble, and Adie felt proud of
a brother distinguished by sentiments so honourable.

Then his eye fell again on the money. It lay
glittering on the table, representing a really
large area of enjoyment.

"Five pounds," he said. "I wonder how long
it is since I had five pounds? Not since I was
at Oxford, I believe. Look here, Adie, what are
you going to do with it all?"

"It is for housekeeping."

"Yes, you must take care not to have any

more money from Dr. Chacomb. I will make a note of the amount."

He took out his pocket-book, and entered it, date and all, with solicitude.

Adie looked guiltily on.

"Oh, I wish I hadn't taken it! I will tell Marion when she comes home, and we will send it back. Fred, it was very wrong of me."

"N-no," said her brother, "I don't think that is necessary. Adie, it just occurs to me that I owe a little bill at the Sheaf for billiards and things; and there is my account at the tobacconist's; and I want a new pair of gloves, and my boots are giving out. There is a sovereign, too—a debt of honour—which I ought to pay; and I should like to buy something for you—it is a long time since I gave you anything, my dear sister; and—and I think it would be best to pay off all these things at once."

He laid his hands upon the whole heap of money, and kept them there.

"O, Fred, not *all!*"

The girl's look, and the tone of entreaty, spoke a whole volume of woman's endurance and man's selfishness.

"Four pounds will do, Adie. That leaves you, you see, one pound five shillings, counting what Marion gave you—more than a whole week's housekeeping in advance. Better say nothing to Marion about the money; and tell Dr. Chacomb, with my compliments, that I am going to repay his small temporary loan with interest—compound interest—when I get a post."

He dropped the sovereigns in his waistcoat pocket and went away, leaving Adie rather sick at heart, and perhaps a little confused between the delicate distinctions of the code of honour which permitted her brother to borrow without repaying, but forbade his taking what was offered.

The woman waiting for Marion crossed the street when she left the house, and stood before her. She was a woman who might be of any age from five and thirty to fifty, with a face which was pretty once, and eyes which formerly might have been bright. She was thin, careworn, and poorly dressed. As she stood waiting her lips moved—she was talking to herself. As

Fred had remarked, her appearance, whether regarded as a pensioner or not, was disreputable.

Marion turned pale when the creature confronted her.

"You promised me you would not molest me. You promised I should never see you at all," she cried. "Why can you not write, as you engaged to do, to the post-office? How dare you come to my very door?"

"I saw him," she replied, "at the window. What a handsome boy it is! Ah me, where did he get his curls from? Where did he get his dimpled chin and his bright eyes? Tell me that, Marion Revel."

"Remember, if you break your contract—if you venture to speak to either of them, if you let them suspect who and what you are—I will help you no more, and you may do your very worst."

"Tell me how *she* is," asked the woman. " I did not see her."

"Adrienne is well and happy—at least, as happy as our poverty will allow."

"I have not caught a glimpse of her for three

months. I hoped that to-day she would put
her pretty face at the window just for me to see
it again. Oh me, oh me! Last Christmas Day
it was I saw her coming home from church with
a girl—quite a girl of the lower classes. Such a
difference as there was between Adrienne, as
tall and straight as a poplar, with a face like a
countess—where did she get her face and figure
from? tell me that—and the little chit with her,
all dimples and curls and chubby cheeks! Such
a contrast; a beautiful contrast for me to look
at! Marion Revel, you never could have had
such a figure, not when you were at your very
best, four years ago; and now you've gone off
sadly, poor thing! All your good looks gone,
like me. It's dreadful to think how care
and trouble spoil a woman's figure. That's
where men have the great advantage over us
women. Why, if it had not been for all my
troubles, I should have been a lovely woman
still."

"Our sins make our troubles," said Marion.

"Do they? Then, Marion Revel, you must
have been a greater sinner than anybody would
think."

"Come," said Marion, "I cannot waste my time. What do you want with me?"

"Money, of course. What else can I want?"

"I have no money. I sent you ten shillings last week. I cannot afford to give you more than five shillings a week. If I give you more, it is robbing *them*."

"And if it is robbing them, it is all in the family, Marion."

Marion shuddered.

"There are others besides them to consider. Look at that finger." She held out her left-hand ring. "What does that mean? Turn over in your mind what that means, and let me know what you are going to do."

"Where is the money gone that I gave you last week? Tell me the truth."

"Yes, there is no reason why I should tell you any lies about it. It is all spent except twopence. And the rent to pay. How is it spent? It is spent on myself. What did I buy with it? I bought bloaters and bread for the boy to eat, and gin for myself to drink. What do I want more for? To buy more bloaters and bread to eat, and more gin to drink. I've had a misfortune, too. Rickety Jem was knocked down by a cab as he was selling papers in Fleet-street, and he's so bruised that he can't walk. Poor little Jem! It's a creditable thing for me, isn't it, to have a son selling *Echoes* for a halfpenny? Give me some money and let me go, Marion Revel."

"I have only sixpence."

"Then give me that, and send me some more."

Marion took out her purse.

"The purse would pawn for eightpence," said the woman. "Give me that too."

"No, I shall not. Here is the sixpence."

"And you talk about being poor! Why, the things you've got on you could put in for at least thirty shillings. There's the malachite cross, that's good for three-and-six. There's the jacket; why, any one would lend you ten shillings on the jacket. There's your gloves —real kid; well, they is patched a bit, and wouldn't fetch much. And your gown! Marion Revel, it's disgraceful if you don't give me more than sixpence, with a whole fortune on your back. I thought your father's daughter was not so selfish."

"How dare you name my father?" cried Marion, roused to frenzy by the dreadful importunity of the woman. "How dare you let the name of Captain Revel pass your lips? Now do your worst, if you dare. Go up and tell that innocent girl who and what you are. Make her more unhappy than she is—it is the utmost that you can do. Do this if you please; but if you do I will give you nothing—nothing. Now let me go."

The beggar began to whimper and cry, using the corner of her shawl in lieu of a pocket handkerchief to mop up imaginary tears.

"You're the only friend I've got in the world," she moaned, "and you throw me over because you are afraid I shall tell. Is it likely I should tell? Do you think I am going to give up five shillings a week? Marion Revel, is it likely, I ask you? And the boy ill at home, and crying for food, and I've got no money. Oh! oh! oh!"

"What shall I do? What am I to do with you?" cried the poor girl, in despair. "Is there no work for women in the world?"

"It depends," the other replied. "For such as you there is work and pay; for such as me there is only work and starvation. I can make cardboard boxes, and get two and twopence, bar stoppages, for twelve hours' work. That is all I can do. Just now there are too many of us wanting to make cardboard boxes, and I can't even get that; so I must come to you and beg. Get me some more money, Marion Revel?"

"If I do, you will only ask for more again when that is gone."

"Yes, I shall. I shall go on begging till I die. I wish I was dead. I wish I was laid in my workhouse grave and all my troubles over. But what would become of the boy?"

Marion sighed heavily.

"I will try and get you some money. If I can, I will bring it myself this afternoon. If I fail, you must try something else."

"I might go on the parish—that would be a fitting end to it all. Sometimes I think I will go and steal something. Marion Revel, I can hurt you in more ways than you think of if I like. I can do worse than tell *them* the truth.

I can go before a magistrate for petty larceny,
and give my real name and history. Mind you,
I never lost my real name; I can bear it still if
I like. So can the boy — little Rickety Jem.
How would you like that?"

The woman passed from whining to threaten-
ing, and back again. She was uncertain in her
behaviour. She alternated between the burden
of her misery, which made her whine, and the
feeling of the hold she possessed over the girl,
which made her threaten. Either weapon was
equally efficacious; for the blow which she could
inflict was not upon Marion, but upon the other
two.

"I can do no more," Marion said. "Go
away and leave me. You have made me unhappy enough. I have told you what I will
try to do, and what I shall do if you dare
to injure those who are dear to me. Now
go."

The woman pulled her shawl closer round her
and flitted away. When she got round the
nearest corner, she looked about her. There
was, of course, a public-house in the street.
There are always in London two things in full

view—a public-house and a church. The population may be broadly divided into two great classes—of those who worship at the former and at the latter place. The woman belonged to those who worshipped at the bar. She made sure that Marion was not looking after her, and crept into the place that is open all day long, a pit for those who like to tumble in. A moment afterwards she came out, wiping her mouth; but she bore herself more upright, and faced the world with a brighter air.

This was Marion's secret—the secret she had discovered on going through her father's papers, the thing she had to keep away from her brother and sister, and to hide from all the world. The knowledge of it made her ashamed; the thought of it weighed her down; the burden of it kept her in the poverty of misery, when she might have been in the poverty of simple comfort.

The woman was, as Fred idly put it, her pensioner—not by choice, but by a dreadful necessity. She had to be kept from starvation for the sake of the dead man lying in Comb Leigh churchyard, and for the sake of the two " children," who knew nothing of it. We have to bear our troubles as we can; but Marion's burden was all the harder because it was so much heavier than her brother or sister were able to suspect.

CHAPTER VI.

HAVING no more money, Marion had to walk, carring her parcel of paintings. From the Tottenham-court-road to Waterloo Bridge is a long step; of that, however, she thought little, provided only she could sell her pictures. The man she was going to had already bought one or two sketches, small things, and at a moderately low price. He lived in Stamford-street, and called himself, on a brass plate, picture dealer and restorer. He was a German by birth, but had been long enough in England to speak English fluently, with only the sweet German accent, so as to interchange a few of the consonants, such as the labials and dentals, in that remarkable and pleasing manner peculiar to his countrymen. His name was Gott-

fried Hermann, and he was said to be de-
scended from the children of Israel, which is
by itself a passport to everybody's favour. As
for his religious principles, they were no doubt
deep and genuine, the result of profound in-
vestigation and anxious thought; but as his
daily practices were beyond everything scoun-
drelly, and his walk, or rather his creeping, in
life was mean, tortuous, and shady, it would be
perhaps superfluous to inquire into his creed.
The Americans—a much more practical people
than ourselves—make it a rule never to ask after
the religion of a stranger. They like, on the other
hand, first to make sure of his honesty. Perhaps
we shall some time or other adopt this, among
a few other laudable Transatlantic customs.

In every profession there must be perforce
some whose natural place is about the lowest
steps. We have not all of us learned to climb.
To some of us climbing is not agreeable, to
others it does not seem profitable. Mr. Gottfried Hermann was one of those who stand
about the lowest steps of picture dealing. He
was also one to whom that position was the
most pleasant. On the higher levels he would

have found the air too bracing, the wind too
keen, the light too brilliant, the situation too
exposed, the sensation to a retiring and sensitive
man suggestive of standing in a pillory.   For
his own part, he preferred to work in the dark,
or rather in a sort of twilight of his own creat-
ing.

He was a fat, round-faced man of fifty, with
a certain stamp upon his expression which,
rightly or wrongly, we are accustomed to regard as indicative of habitual self-indulgence.
He smoked a great-bowled German pipe, which
might hold half an ounce or so, all day long;
and he sat at the front window of his house in
Stamford-street contemplating the passers-by
when he was not studying a picture.   There
grew up from the area a thin and skeleton-
like vine, which threw its slender arms across
his window, and gave an air of verdure and
Eden-like innocence to his features, as they
beamed behind the sickly leaves in summer.
In winter the tree suggested the similitude of
the spider in his web.

This morning, the leaves being not yet out,
and only a green budding visible along the

branches, he had the spidery look as his flabby face shone through the panes. He was not alone. A man in the last depths of shabbiness was with him, standing hat in hand, a suppliant.

"Give me work, Mr. Hermann. I can do it well and quickly."

"Tell me about New York first, what you was doing there."

"I was copying there."

"Aha! he was gopying. Zo, what was he gopying?"

This impudent rascal habitually adopted the use of the third person in talking to those who asked for work, with the deliberate intention of insulting his visitors, and an inward chuckle at the thought that most of them did not know they were being treated as servants, and were too miserable to resent it if they did.

"I was with Messrs. Fourbe, Gredin, and Fripon, the largest picture dealers in America."

"I know them, I know them. Let him sit down and tell me all he can about their business."

"There is not much to tell. They had good

copies of pictures made in Rome, Dresden, and Florence, and their chief business was to have more copies made from them."

"And they sold them as originals. Most unbrinzibled."

"No, they were sold as genuine copies by good living artists, made on the spot. It is a safer business. They used to have a canvas stretched on the wall, and I and two or three others copied all day, as quickly as we could. As fast as the pictures were finished, they were cut out and framed. Mostly they were sold by auction. I've got a very rapid hand, sir."

"Goarse," Mr. Hermann replied. "Ferry goarse, that kind of work."

"You see, sir, copying does not require the fine painting, Mr. Gredin used to say, that is expected in an original."

Mr. Hermann shook his head.

"Go away. I give you ten days. Make me a—a—a—let me see—a Greuze; you can do all styles, ja wohl. Yes, a Greuze, and—and I shall see. What is this?"

He took a picture that was standing with its face to the wall, and laid it on the table.

"That is a Linnell."

"Is it a gopy or is it an original?"

"If it was anywhere but here, I should say it was an original," replied the man. "I know enough of the trade to be quite sure that it is not an original, or else it would not be here."

"Ha! ha! He is right, this fellow. He is right. Let him go away now, and come back in ten days with the Greuze."

The man left him, and Mr. Hermann watched him down the steps.

"Ah, he is poor. He has done someding. I will find out what. Himmel, here is the pewtiful young lady, Miss Reffel. I am glad she did not meet that other poor teffel."

He saw Marion coming up to his door, and went to open it himself.

"Gott pless me!" he cried; "it's Miss Reffel. Come, my tear young lady, come in. What a bleasure to see you, and what a plessing to know that you are well! Come in, and show me what you have prought me. It will be coot; oh, it will be coot. I know that it will be coot. There—sit down. You may look at the bictures while we talk. There's a pewtiful thing, now.

Give me the liddle barcel—zo—yes—zo. What do you think of that for a real and genuine Linnell—a rare and pewtiful Linnell?"

It was a delicious, soft, warm, sunlit scene—a field of standing corn, with a tree at the right hand, and a wood behind. Creeping up in the background, a thunder-cloud.

"It is a very nice picture," said Marion; "but it looks to me like a copy."

He laid down Marion's parcel unopened, and held the picture to the light.

"A gopy!" he jerked out, angrily. "A gopy! Why does she think it is a gopy?"

"Perhaps I am wrong," Marion replied; "but I should have said, on looking at it, that there could be no doubt about its being a copy. However, if you are sure—"

"If I am sure!" he echoed. "Why, if I am not sure, who the teffel can be sure? I beg your bardon, young lady, but if there ever was a genuine Linnell—why, there—never mind; let us look at the things in the liddle barcel."

He opened it, and began to turn over the pictures one by one, talking all the time as he held them to the light.

"I don't want to buy any more bictures. I think I shall never buy any more so long as I live. There's more bictures bainted than beoble to buy them. Times are ferry hard, Miss Reffel."

"Indeed they are, Mr. Hermann, else I should not be here; but you must buy mine, if you please, because I want some money."

"Flowers and fruit. Yes, ferry bretty—ferry bretty inteet. But no one looks at flowers and fruit now. It is a real bity to see a young lady of your talent waste her brecious time over flowers and fruit. You might as well go to the Zoological Cardens and baint the monguies. It would be pedder to baint the monguies. Beoble like monguies, and they don't like flowers and fruit. One, two, three—three bictures of beaches and crapes. What shall we say for this boor lot altogether?"

"I was thinking of a guinea a-piece," said Marion, humbly.

Mr. Hermann held up his hands in a kind of horror.

"A kuinea?—twenty-one shillings a-piece for liddle things like those? My tear young lady—

oh, tear! oh, tear! It's ferry difficult to refuse a sweet young bainter like you. Why am I not a rich man? What shall I say to this young lady? Miss Reffel, if I was to give you a whole kuinea a-piece for these liddle pictures, I should be a ruined man. I should have to go back to my liddle vife and my liddle children in Jairmany mit nozing. Gottfried Hermann would be pangrupt."

He emphasized his assertion with many and weighty gestures of his fat white hands, and much nodding of his very large head.

"Then what could you give me?" asked Marion. "Please remember, Mr. Hermann, that I am very poor, and that you are—"

"Ferry poor too—oh, yes!—ferry, ferry poor, I am. Come, let us regon up together. I shall keep these liddle bictures in my place for two years; then they will go to America; they will be framed; there will be the gommission. It's the gommission zuks away the brovit. Ah, if only we could do without the gommission—those wicked sgoundrels! Now, let us see. I keep the bictures two years, say fife shillings interest—that is nozing; dey go to America

wit lots of others, say fife shillings more ; fram-
ing, fife shillings more ; gommission, ten shillings ; there is twenty-five shillings : profit to
myself — I am ferry poor, Miss Reffel — five
shillings, that's all. What is a poor liddle five
shillings? But it is all to oblige you, my tear
girl. Ah, I would lose eferything to oblige
a young lady, and a sweet bainter like you.
That's thirty shillings. Suppose they give in
New York—bicture dealers are an unbrinzibled
lot—most unbrinzibled " (he shook his head,
as though he and his English brethren were
models of virtue and honesty)—"suppose they
give us forty shillings; that's the outside
figure. I will risk that, Miss Reffel, to oblige
you ; and it makes—ja, zo—yoost ten shillings
a-piece."

He took out his purse and counted out three
half-sovereigns, which he pushed over to Marion.

"It seems very little," she said. "Could you
not—"

"My tear young lady, you have seen the
figures—be reasonable."

The sight of the money was a temptation not

to be resisted. She took up the three little gold
pieces, and put them in her purse.

The honest Mr. Hermann went on with his
examination of the other pictures.

"Scene by the seaside—zo; light a little too
strong—yes. A head—zo." It was the head
of Adrienne. "Where did you get this face?
Did you draw it from vancy, or did you gopy
it? Is it a bortrait?"

"It is my sister."

"Himmel!" he replied, with a glittering eye.
"Her sister—it is her sister! What a face!
what a pewtiful face! Young lady, I will give
you a whole kuinea for this bicture. I will
give you a kuinea for every one that you baint
like it. Ah, what a face! It is a Fenus—mein
Gott, a new Fenus. Make me more of her,
make me lots of her, and you shall make a
liddle vortune out of your zister. Bring her
here to me to talk mit me; I should like to see
this lovely Fenus, this young Miss Reffel. Is
she a bainter too? Bring her to me."

Marion hesitated for a moment, but she took
the guinea. After all, it was money, and she
wanted it.

"Zo"—he pushed aside the water-colours.

"You have forgotten the seaside piece," said Marion.

It was so—the forgetful Mr. Hermann had pushed this with the rest into his portfolio.

"Ah, yes—zo; I had forgotten. Let me have this liddle bicture with the rest, Miss Reffel, because I am so ferry poor."

"No," said Marion, strictly; "give me a guinea for that picture, or I will take it away. Why, there are four days' work in that picture."

"Four days only! and she asks a kuinea— nearly two kuineas a week! What a grand thing to be a water-golour bainter! Two kuineas a week! I will gif vifteen shillings for it."

"No."

"Then seventeen. Come, Miss Reffel, come. We are old friends."

"No; let me have it back; and let me go."

He took it out, and held it up. It was a pretty little thing—a reminiscence of Comb Leigh, with the water dancing in the little cove, the brambles climbing over the rocks, and on the left the old carpenter cobbling the bottom of the boat, while his tar-pot sent up its straight,

thin column of smoke, marring where it ascended the clear blue of the sky. It was more
than pretty, as the dealer saw; it had feeling
and truth in it, as well as beauty; it was a picture which, if it had a good name at the back
of it, would be worth thirty or forty pounds at
least.

Mr. Hermann placed it back in his portfolio.

"I suppose I must," he said; "a young lady
always does what she likes with me. Here is
a kuinea, and I shall have to save and scrabe
to make it up. Baint me more heads, Miss
Reffel, of your sister. Baint her in gostume.
She would do for Haidée; she would do for
Marcuerite; she would do for—mein Gott! how
she *would* do for Codifa. Baint her in dress
and out of dress, and I will gif you a kuinea for
efery one, efery one—a whole kuinea. I will."

"My sister is not a model, Mr. Hermann."

"Then make her a mottel. Why is she not a
mottel?" he replied, angrily. "If she is ferry
poor, and you are ferry poor, why is she not
a mottel? You may as well be a mottel as
starve, I suppose."

As Mr. Hermann in his younger days had **sat**

in the Life School himself, he thought strongly on the subject of models. Moreover, as his wife, his mother, his sisters, and in fact his whole family, had been in the profession, it was not likely that he would hear the calling spoken of slightingly.

"I hope we shall not starve," said Marion. "Thank you, Mr. Hermann. May I bring you any other pictures, even if I do not paint my sister's face again?"

"I could put you in the way," said Mr. Hermann, looking musingly at the girl—"I could put you in the way of making a large sum of money; oh, a ferry large sum of money."

"How could I do that—by painting?"

"Yes, by bainting; only it must be by bainting things for me. When pictures are ordered, I must have them bainted, and I think you could baint them well. That Linnell was bainted for me by a young man I know; and yet, you see, you found it out at once."

"I thought you said it was genuine?"

"So I did, so I did; but that was only to try you. Now, young lady, I will tell you some of the real secrets of the bicture trade, and then you can make money for yourself. I am always generous with the young ladies. I would do anything for the young ladies—anything in the wide, wide world; and I am going to put a fortune in your hands—a fortune—if you can work it properly."

"I am sure I am very grateful."

"Now, listen; don't inderrupt. That Linnell —how was it done? My young man goes to an exhibition, and then to a private gallery, and then to Ghristie's, and so on—wherever they have got any Linnells. He is not allowed to sit down and make a gopy, so he takes the gadalok, and, when nopody is looging, he draws a tree from this bicture, and a field from that, and a bit of field flower from another, and then, my tear, he goes home, my young man does, and he makes a Linnell by himself, all gomplede—a new Linnell, that Mr. Linnell himself would not know from one of his own, made up of liddle bits taken from half a dozen bictures he bainted himself; and then he brings it to me, this gleffer young man, and if the bicture is well done, and deceives a stranger, I gif him

—I gif him fife pounds for that bicture—fife pounds, young lady."

" And what do you do with it?"

" What do I do with it? I sell it, my tear, I sell it to the bicture tealers, who sell it to other bicture tealers, and it goes round the trade, and then about the world. Mein Gott! if all the calleries in Manchester and America were emptied, there would be more Linnells and Codmans than fifty men could baint in fifty years. And such a lot done by my young men—oh, such a lot! I've got the glefferest young men you effer saw. Not this one," he pointed to the ' Linnell' which lay on the table. " He shall go—he shall go to the teffel; he used to baint well, but he has done bad lately. I am afraid he is a young man of bad morals. I think he trinks."

" What you want me to do," said Marion, who had grown very pale, " is, as I understand, to go round the exhibitions and sale-rooms, take a bit from one picture, and a bit from another, patch up the whole in a single painting, and call it after a modern artist."

" That is it, my tear young lady; that is yoost what I want."

"Then, Mr. Hermann," she said, "you are a villain."

"Eh? mein Gott! Miss Reffel!"

He laid down his pipe, and looked at the girl with feigned surprise.

"I say you are a dishonest, wicked man, Mr. Hermann. I will have no dealings with you. Give me back my pictures, and take your money, and let me go. Give me back my pictures."

She laid her hand on the portfolio.

"Not so fast, Miss Reffel—not so fast. The bictures are mine; I have bought them. I shall not give them back."

"Then, Mr. Hermann, I will tell everybody who you are. I will warn the world against you."

"Who will you tell?" he asked, a shade of anxiety crossing his face. "Who will you tell, Miss Reffel?"

"I will tell Mr. Burls, the picture dealer."

He burst into loud laughter.

"She will tell Purls! Ho! ho! ho! She is going to tell Purls! Eh, my tear, how Purls will be astonished! I suppose never was a man

so astonished as Purls will be astonished. Purls
the honest, Purls the truthful! Eh, mein Gott!
what a plow it will be to Purls! Go and tell
Purls, my tear; go and tell Purls immediately."

He laughed again. The idea of Mr. Burls
being told was too much for him.

"Go and tell all the tealers, Miss Reffel. Ah,
they will be almost as much astonished as Mr.
Purls—good Mr. Purls! Ho! ho! ho!"

Marion had no reply to make.

"Gome, my pretty young lady--gome, Miss
Reffel, do not be angry about nozings. Sit
down again. Most of my young men go off the
same way when they first hear my plan. Then
they get poorer and poorer, and then they gome
to me to get rich. Sit down and listen; only
one moment. See, the Manchester men want
bictures; the stockbrokers and the goddon-
brokers want bictures; the New York merchants
want bictures. They can't all have bictures;
they won't have gopies; but they don't know
bictures. Then they go to the tealers, and the
tealers go to each other, and one after the other
they come to Gottfried Hermann. They come
to me. I am the benefactor of the world.

Wherefer the English language is spoken—
wherefer there are rich beoble who want bictures, there you will find the works of my young
men. Without me bictures by modern masters
would be so tear, that they would haf to puy
bictures from the liddle sgrubs. Think of that.
By my help the goddon-brokers look at their
walls and say, 'That is a Linnell;' ho! ho! 'That
is an Eddy;' ha! ha! 'Here is a Leighdon, and
there is a Roberts.' Won't you sit down, Miss
Reffel, and listen quietly? You are such a ferry
nice girl, that I should not like to see you go off
in a rage.

"The best of it is," he went on, "that they
puy the bictures because they think it is a goot
infestment of their money. Ho! ho! They
leafe them in their last wills and destamens to
their heirs as ferry precious broberty. Ha! ha!
But when they are sent up to Ghristie's, they
are sometimes found out, and the heirs are sold.
Ho! ho! ho! what an infestment of money—eh?
It serves them right, because if they would buy
the bictures of young artists like yourself, Miss
Reffel, they would get the falue of their money.
They would—mein Gott, they would. Sit down,

young lady, and listen to me. Don't go away in a rage."

"I will hear no more," said Marion. "Find some one else to work your cheats for you."

"You will come back, young lady—you will come back. You will get no one to give you such a goot price for your bictures as Gottfried Hermann; you will come then, and work with my young men, and make pewtiful Eddys and Leighdons and Linnells. Oh, yes; you will come back in a liddle time; you will come back to your friend, and I bear you no malice, my tear young lady—no malice at all. I like you for it; I do indeed. Good-bye, Miss Reffel. Oh," he cried, as she left the room, "do baint your sister for me in oils; baint her as Cotifa, and I will gif you ten pounds. I will indeed— ten pounds, mein Gott—ten pounds! How pewtiful she would look as Cotifa!"

CHAPTER VII.

ARION was more than outraged by the proposals of this unholy alien, this German producer of new and original pictures — she was humiliated. If you want to humiliate your enemy beyond endurance, ask him to do something which shows the very small respect in which you hold him. To the frailer vessels of humanity, indeed — those of ornamented porcelain and coloured glass—it is worse to be asked to do things dishonourable than it is actually to do them. Men who negotiate foreign loans, men who bull and bear the stock market, men who promote bubble companies, 'salt' mines, draw up prospectuses, advertise sherry, send ships to sea that are bound to sink, direct bankrupt life insurance associations, 'adapt' plays, and abuse their rivals in anonymous criticism,—all these can bear their heads proudly, and believe themselves honourable and upright men. Ask them confidentially to join in cracking a crib, fencing a wipe, or any of the humbler and less remunerative forms of treachery, and lo! their self-respect collapses like a pricked balloon. For a discreditable proposal implies discredit. Marion had borne a great deal without repining. She worked all day for a miserable pittance; she saw others reap the fruits of her labours: this was all part of the condition of poverty; it did not make her seriously unhappy. Never before this had she been asked to join in fraud; never before this had the sweet waters of Hope in her heart been troubled by such a prophecy as Mr. Hermann's, that she would come back soon, poorer than ever, and be glad to take his offer.

Should she ever go back so ruined and lost as to accept the foul proposal? Were there, then, such depths of misery as would drive the unfortunate to give up even the semblance of honour? Was it hopeless to struggle with the world? And were all the avenues barred by the middle-

man, to rob and plunder those who must sell or
starve?

Alas, how many have given an answer! Ask
of the middle-man, if he will tell you. Look
behind the curtain, the kindly veil which hides
the dreadful features of truth. See at their toil
the slaves of those who take the work and sell
it, and grow fat upon the proceeds. There are
such fat and noisome grubs in literature, but it
is in art that they chiefly flourish. They starve
the struggling artist into submission; they cheat
and plunder him; they lie to him, and steal
from him; and when his last spark of ambition
is extinct, they make him the instrument of
their forgeries. It is no fiction, but a miserable
truth, that Gottfried Hermann exists and drives
a roaring trade, keeping in his pay the men who
have been starved and cheated by Burls. The
middle-man bars all the avenues.

For the moment, Marion felt as if she was in
the bonds of a stern necessity which was drag-
ging her downwards, and there seemed no escape. It was in vain that she fought against
the feeling. It seemed that the man spoke
truly of coming events. She would have to go

back and humbly ask for work—work of any kind, in order that she and hers might eat a morsel of bread. And there came upon her brain, for a while, the black pall of despair, when the mind is shrouded with darkness that can be felt; when the distinction between good and evil, for which Adam gave up Paradise, is lost again, and the earth seems to be hell; when there is no more hope, and the voice of God is silent.

She would have to go back. She shuddered at thinking of his soft and flabby face, his fat white hands, his oily voice. It came upon her quite suddenly what he meant by asking her to paint her sister for him—girls do not understand these things at first. The thought was like a shower bath. She shook herself together, and dared once more to resolve. Never, come what might—poverty, disappointment, distress—never would she go back to that man again.

She had wandered, wrapped in her gloomy thoughts, as far as the Horse Guards, when this sudden rage seized her. She crossed the road, and went into St. James's Park. The sun was shining—it had been shining in the streets, in-

deed, but poor Marion did not notice it there.
Here it fell among the young leaves of April,
and flashed a twinkling, fitful light, unlike the
steady glow upon the foliage of summer, on the
bushes and shrubs putting on their brand-new
spring apparel.   Here, too, the wild ducks, who
habitually take up their winter residence, because
it is a safe and secluded spot, in St. James's
Park, were reminding each other of important
appointments at the back of the north wind,
made eight months before in those iceless seas
where the secret of the Pole is hidden ; the
swans were beginning the soft nothings which
precede their brief-lived marriage ties ; and the
sparrows, who are a practical folk, as a rule, and
always intent on business, were feeling the soft
influence of the season, as well as Marion and
the nursemaids, who had the park to themselves.
She turned to the left, and walked along the
banks of the lake, while calmer and more hopeful thoughts gradually came back to her.   Her
hands, which had been tightly locked, unclasped,
and she looked around her.   After all, whatever
happened, they were not utterly destitute.   She
had her fifty pounds a year, enough to give her

some little standpoint from which to resist the
enemy. They were cast down, but not utterly
forsaken; by some means or other she should
contrive, and perhaps— But she checked the
rising hope that perhaps something would turn
up. That is only the hope of a helpless person.
However, perhaps her own picture—the thing
into which she had thrown all her soul and all
her powers—might somehow advance her. Of
course, she never entertained the least trust in
the promises and expectations of her brother.
She was the family bread-winner; he was the
family spendthrift. It was all part of the great
Providential design: some families have an in-
valid; some have one of weak intellect; hers
had one who could not work. In fact, it had
two; but poor Adie, who could not make money,
had her functions, and kept house for them all.
I feel almost ashamed to add what is so appa-
rent to all, that Fred's helplessness in no way
diminished Marion's affection for him. It had
even ceased to irritate her. She made a never-
ending series of excuses for him; he was her
charge; it was her duty to work for him.

Perhaps it was the soft spring air that brought

Marion's thoughts back to a peaceful channel; perhaps, too, it was the sunshine and the warmth that made her think of Gerald, long lost, and that short love chapter in her life. Some people like a novel that is all love; I am sure a life ought to be all love, and especially that love which cannot be written in a book, the best love of all, which follows the short-lived fever of passion. The memory of Marion's brief romance left its enduring mark upon her mind, making her softer, more womanly, more open to sympathy, more ready to pity and forgive. That is love's special function. Those who cannot love are cruel, selfish, and unfeeling, like Narses. Those who can, very likely have every kind of vice, but they have the possibilities of affection, which means self-denial. "Joys," said Blake, painter and poet, "impregnate." The fruits of even short-lived happiness are tenderness, thought for others, and the gracious sacrifice of labour. Among women, those are best who have been loved and have loved; among men, those are best who have staked their happiness upon the faith and truth of a woman. You stake your love, perhaps, and lose, but oftener you win; and always you are a gainer for having dared to stake.

Marion paced the gravel backwards and forwards, thinking of these things. Presently she became aware of a heavy step behind her. The step seemed familiar; it drew up to her, and she saw that it belonged to Dr. Chacomb.

"I saw you," he said, "as I was on my way to the hospital. May we have a little talk?"

"If you will only talk about—if you will only not talk—" said Marion, thinking of the last night's conversation.

The doctor bowed gravely.

"You have only to express a wish, Miss Revel," he said; "besides," he added, airily, "the time has not come round yet."

"The time?"

"Yes. I began to think it possible six months ago. I asked you then. You said, No. I asked you again last night. You said, No. I shall ask you again in a little while—"

"And I must say No then. Oh, Dr. Chacomb, do not ask me again."

"I must, Miss Revel. If you say No, I shall ask again, and again after that. I do not despair. You have owned that you do not dislike me. I trust to time, though a man can ill afford time at nine and forty. Meanwhile, I am consoling myself with hard work."

"I am glad that you are succeeding."

"Thank you. Trust me, dear Miss Revel, that I shall not obtrude my suit upon you more than I can help."

If the man would only not make such speeches! Who could help being irritated with him?

Marion turned the conversation.

"Tell me about your hospital."

"Would you be interested to hear about it? Let us sit down. There is a seat, and I really do think the east winds have gone at last. Now, what shall I tell you? I had an inspiration, as the French say—they are very profane, the French. I saw there was no hospital for gout. I saw that the best way for a physician to get himself a practice was to start a hospital. I borrowed money of Chauncey Chacomb, my cousin, and I started mine."

This statement was not strictly accurate. He should have said that he had taken money from

Chauncey Chacomb, inasmuch as he was receiver of the rents, and accounted to nobody.
A dishonest receiver might have pocketed the
whole. Dr. Chacomb, wiser than the Unjust
Steward of the parable, frankly confessed that he
borrowed the money. The fact of the lender
not being consulted was, of course, of no con-
sequence.

"I borrowed money from poor Chauncey," he
said, "and I started this hospital. It is now
in full swing. Out-patients in the morning, seen
by my assistants; in-patients visited every day
by myself, physician-in-chief; and private patients received at the institution itself, as well as
in Adelaide-street, Carnarvon-square. The hospital is supported by voluntary contributions.
Some day I will show you the prospectus, drawn
up by the secretary—a clever fellow: I picked
him up cheap—who might have done great
things in literature but for his unfortunate crook
of the elbow. As he only crooks it at night, it
does not matter to the hospital; and I take care
to keep him poor."

"And you are now a great physician?"

"Hum! I should say Yes to anybody but

12—2

yourself. But you, Miss Revel, are a sort of touchstone. I like to tell you the exact truth. I am not a great physician—there are no great physicians; but I have learned things of late, and I am as good as any of my brethren—a good deal better than Dr. Porteous, of Savile-row, who pretends—the pompous old donkey!—to be the leader in gout. Wait a year or two, till I have snuffed him out."

He snorted, and looked as angry as a writer whose pet field has been invaded.

"I am sure you are a good physician."

"I use new medicines, and they say I am a quack. Quack! quack! quack! Any man can say that. I do not follow the English Pharma-copœia, and I am not too proud to learn from other people. I chalk out my own line. Medi-cine in this country, my dear young lady, is dead; the doctors are smitten with the disease of stupidity. They neither inquire, nor invent, nor experiment. They do not dare try a fresh drug."

"Perhaps it is as well not to try things that have no properties."

"Nonsense! Everything has properties, if you

can find them out. The dandelion and the
nettle, the buttercup and daisy, have properties,
if you analyze them. But the doctors cannot
analyze. Every weed in the hedge has properties, but we are afraid to move a step to find
them out. Do you think Nature makes things
just to look pretty? If you want to know what
herbs are worth, you must go, not to the
botanists, who are only able to give you the
Latin names; nor to the doctors, because they
will say that the plant is not in the Pharma-
copœia; but to the old women of the villages,
and gather their knowledge. We are getting so
civilized that we must be cured as we are taught,
by books. The old women are fallen into dis-
repute; they die, and their knowledge dies with
them—more's the pity! But they *know*."

"And you have consulted them?"

"I have gone about picking up hints," he replied, "and I have learned things. I have found
old women who can do with foxglove, henbane,
hawksweed, and nightshade what we doctors
cannot do with all the nastiness compounded at
the wholesale chemists', and sold at a profit of a
thousand per cent. My old women learned the

art from their mothers, who learned it from theirs, and so on, till we get to the Witch of Endor. As for her, I have myself sat at the feet of the Witch of Endor, only my old woman never heard of Samuel, and therefore could not call him up. I would have asked her to, by gad! like a bird, if I thought Samuel knew anything about drugs for gout."

"Then you ought to cure everybody," said Marion.

"No. There is a time for every man when, by the rules of his constitution, he is bound to die. No doctor can stave off that day; all he can do is to prolong life till the day comes. My patients want to be told their time. I pretend to know it, and I refuse to tell them. I am, of course, a great humbug. Men ought to live their appointed time, and then die of old age. Medicine is not of much use—it can only help you on to your limit; but if you catch one of the big diseases, like cholera, or typhus, or scarlet fever, or diphtheria, off you go, and no doctor in the world can help you.

"Stay," he said; "you said something yesterday about my cousin Chauncey and Gerald. I have got a letter to-day from his housekeeper, a very worthy person, whom I sent down there to look after him. Would you like me to read it to you?"

"Is there anything about Gerald in it?"

"Now, my dear Miss Revel, how can there be? Is it likely? Pray believe me when I assure you that if I heard anything about Gerald, even though it were to destroy my own hopes, I would tell you immediately. But I shall not. Poor Gerald!"

He shook his head solemnly, and opened the letter.

"Chauncey is quite sane, except upon one or two points. He is fully persuaded that he murdered your father, and he has little hallucinations on minor subjects, which are of no importance."

They were certainly of no importance to Marion, but they were of considerable importance to Chauncey, inasmuch as they led him to believe that he had no control over his own affairs; that the doctor spent his money for him, ordered his household for him, gave him a housekeeper and a guardian, and administered everything for his own behoof and special advantage.

"You see," he added, "I go down as often as I can—about once a fortnight—to see that the place is kept up."

"Dear Comb Leigh!" murmured Marion—"when shall I see it again?"

"Whenever you like—whenever you like! Nothing in the world could give me greater pleasure than to take you to Chacomb."

"And Mr. Chauncey Chacomb?"

"As if it matters what he thinks about it!"

"Thank you," said Marion. "I do not think I can ever go to Chacomb Hall, after what has happened."

He was a coarse-grained man, this doctor, she thought.

"Well, when you like to come. By the way, do you remember the picture with the back turned outwards? It was the thing that drove Chauncey so wild at the last. He made me say that I agreed with him, and thus your father laughed at him. He has got that picture hanging in his own bed-room now, and he looks at it every day—the back of it, I mean—with the

hope of bringing out the details. Poor Chauncey! He never was a good fellow; and I think
I like him as well now that he is known to be
cracked as when he was only foolish, but considered to be of sound mind."

"But people—his tenants—consider him of
sound mind still, do they not?"

"No; they only pretend to. They know well
enough that he is off his head. We have had to
observe a few precautions— nothing very serious,
but still a few—and they have been noticed.
The housekeeper—a most worthy, estimable
woman—writes to me to-day, and I will read the
letter. I have not had time to look at it yet."

"MY DEAREST JOE"—("I beg your pardon,"
he stopped and choked)—"My dear Dr. Chacomb—It is a fortnight since you were down here,
and I hoped to see you last Saturday"—("I could
not go," he explained, "on account of dear Lady
Strongwater's gout, which threatened to fly to
the stomach; I was up with her all night")—"I
hoped to see you last Saturday. Your patient
has been going on pretty well, though full of
tantrums, as usual. He has been very fractious

for the last week, but he does not want to see
you. In fact, I think, in his present mood, you
had better not come. Last week nothing would
suit him but going to the cliff where the accident
took place. I believe he wanted to roll over
himself. I refused to let him go; so he said he
should wait till midnight, get out of window,
and go and throw himself down where Captain
Revel fell. Then I gave in—had a little party
made up of Jem "—("You remember Bos'n Jem,
Miss Revel")—"Charles, the stable-boy, and myself. We all set off to walk to the cliff together.
Directly we got outside the gates, he said it was
ridiculous, and marched straight back again.
Then he went to the Collection and cried; said
nobody cared for him."—("It is one of the features of hallucination, Miss Revel, that the patient cries if he is put out.")—"I prescribed port
with his dinner, and we got him comfortably
to bed."—("Very good, very good! A bottle of
port is a fine thing for hallucinations. If you
feel low, wind yourself up. Sound medical
maxim.")

"Poor Mr. Chacomb!"

The doctor seemed to forget that he was

reading this interesting epistle aloud, and went on with it.

"In the morning he was quiet, and we had a talk."

Here there was a gap, because the writer had taken another sheet. The doctor looked at this, changed colour violently, and crumpled the letter in his hand.

"Well," he said, with an effort, "there's nothing more—nothing of importance. My poor cousin is hopelessly gone. I shall not lock him up, because he can do no harm where he is, and the treatment I prescribe for him will be best in the long-run. As it is, as it is—" He shrugged his shoulders.

"Yes," said Marion; "when Gerald comes home again he will thank you."

"You think—" he began.

"I am sure. Whenever I think of it, I feel the same assurance. Gerald is coming home. It is impossible that he should be dead, and that I should not know it."

"That is superstition."

"I cannot help it. We feel the presence of the living with us; why should we not feel the fact that they are alive? Gerald is alive at this moment; and I think, because I feel it so much more strongly now than I did a year ago, that he is coming home."

"Good-bye, Miss Revel," said the doctor, abruptly. "Put poor Gerald out of your thoughts, and—if you can—put me, my poor unworthy self, in his place."

He walked down the gravel path with his heavy tread, which was so silent on a carpet, and disappeared.

"What a fool I am! Why should I want to read Julia's letters to Marion without reading them myself first?"

He took the letter out of the envelope again, and read it.

"MY DEAR JOE"—("Hang her!")—"It is a fortnight"—("I read all that to Marion")—"And now I have got something important to tell you. I knew that you would never marry me, in spite of all your promises; and for the last three months Chauncey has been urging me to marry him on the sly. So yesterday we went quietly to the registrar's office, where I had had the

notices put up"—("The deceitful little devil!")—
"and now, if you please, I am Mrs. Chacomb,
of Chacomb Hall, Chacomb."—("The deuce you
are!")

" Chauncey is very good to me. It is all nonsense to say he is mad; he is no more mad than
you, and he declares he will prove it." ("The
devil he will!")—" He is a little flighty at night,
and sees faces in the dark—so would any one
in this lonely house. He hears voices, which
everybody might hear in such a quiet place.
Dear Joe, you know that I never could and
never did love anybody but you; but when this
poor little man kept begging and praying—and
you away in London—and offering to make me
a lady, a real lady, I thought I could do
nothing better than take his offer."—("Nothing
better, ma'am, nothing better; and I'm deuced
glad of it;" but he spoke with a little bitterness.)
—"I do not expect the county ladies"—("Eh?
Ho! ho! the county ladies!")—"will call upon
me] just yet; but I am going to send a notice of
the marriage to the papers, and I can wait. Remember, my dear Joe, for the memory of old
times, my husband and I will always be happy

to see you whenever your professional duties
will allow you to come.—Always your affectionate cousin,

"JULIA CHACOMB."

"The cheek of it!" said the doctor. "The
confounded impudence and cheek! I send her
down to obey my orders, and, by gad, she
marries him! And now she thinks to be the
mistress of Chacomb, does she? We will see,
we will see. Julia, my girl, I've known you in
the ballet, and I've known you in the burlesque;
I've known you on the quiet, and I've known
you on the rampage; but I never knew you to
try such a big game as this before. Never
mind, Mrs. Chauncey Chacomb the second, you
haven't got over Joseph yet. I shall go down
next Saturday and bring this young couple—ho!
ho! he's fifty-eight and she's forty, if she's a day
—to reason. I shall let them know who is the
master of Chacomb. I shall put my foot down.
Very well, Julia—very well."

CHAPTER VIII.

SATURDAY morning was an off-day with Dicky, so far as Mr. Lilliecrip was concerned. He was wont to spend it at the British Museum, in preparation of the articles, paragraphs, and letters which formed his tale of labour for the *Weekly Intelligence* and the *Christian Clerk*. He was awakened by the street cries, which in London do duty for the dogs of rural solitudes and the lark of the poets. He rose hastily, for a thought flashed across him in his dreams, piercing the innermost marrow of his soul.

"Good heavens!" he gasped, rushing his toilet, so to speak—"eight o'clock already; and to-morrow is Sunday. Never mind, I may be in time yet."

He did not, as when we saw him last, waste

time in lamenting or apostrophising the deficiencies of his wardrobe. On the contrary, he huddled everything on as fast as possible, reduced his curly and abundant locks to something like smoothness, and hastened downstairs.

At the door of the ancient dame of whom mention has already been made, he met her granddaughter, Miss Ethelreda Vyvyan, commonly known as "Ready Vyvyan" by those who knew her best, and familiar to public eyes and ears in connection with the Royal Hemisphere Theatre, where she took second parts in burlesques: an accomplished young lady; one who had a strong, if not a melodious voice, and who could be trusted to get through a song without absolutely losing sight of time and tune; who could dance passably; who looked charming in "page" costume—she preferred it "full page," she said; and who was pretty enough for the simple costume of the theatrical, village maiden with short skirts, silk stockings, and a coquettish hat. But she was happiest in a costume *à la Henri Quatre*, which displayed more of the figure than womankind in western

Europe have thought necessary since their con-
version to Christianity. "Popsy," her grand-
mother called her; and what her surname really
was, or her Christian' name either, I am sorry
to say, I do not know. She was carrying the
breakfast milk upstairs, and looked as fresh
and blooming as if she had not come home after
a late supper at two o'clock in the morning.
Seeing the poet, she set down her milk, and
laughed and clapped her hands.

"How are you, Dicky?" she asked, with a
familiarity that spoke of old and confirmed
friendship. "How are you this morning, old
boy? None the worse for last night? Let me
look at you: eyelids rather red, cheeks a little,
twitchy, tongue a little dry—got a fur upon it,
I should think. You've been going it, Dicky
Carew. Coming in to pay poor old granny her
money? Not you."

"The fact is," said Dicky, "that I am going
into the City to draw my dividends."

"Walker!" was the vulgar rejoinder of this
young lady. She accompanied it with a gesture
which we may briefly indicate by saying that it
betrayed a complete mastery over her limbs,

and an early training for the ballet. "Walker! How much do you owe the old lady? Never mind; you'll pay me some day, whenever I'm hard up, and it will wait. I've got lots of money now. I say, Dicky, come and see me to-night. Better! I'll give you a pit ticket. New piece. Heroine jumps from the flies into a cascade of real water. 'Heaven help me, I am lost! Death before dishonour!' So—" She took an imaginary header over the banister, and posed. "Not one of them, not even Dardie Duncan, had the pluck to take it, except me; and, bless you, if you've got good eyes, it's as easy as—as saying you are off to draw your dividends; only it wouldn't do to miss your tip. Better come, Dicky."

"I can't," said Dicky. "I am going to dine this evening with the Countess of Grasmere, else I should be quite at your service."

"Lord! Now I am going to have supper with Prince Bithisnozoff, the Russian swell, and a few of his very particular friends, at the Prætorium, after the curtain drops. Bet you my supper, Dicky, will be a good deal jollier than your dinner. I suppose you'll get new heels to your boots first, and take the swallow-tail out of pawn, for her ladyship's dinner? Good-bye, Dicky."

She disappeared singing the last burlesque melody. A moment afterwards she reappeared.

"Dicky, old boy," she cried after his retreating figure, "I heard you go upstairs last night at half-past one. You only tumbled down— altogether, that is—once and a half, and carried your boots and hat quite safely all the way up. I felt for you, poor fellow! What a dreadful thing to go to bed sober! Haven't you got a bad headache this morning?"

Dicky made no reply, but ran down the stairs.

"She's a remarkable girl, Popsy," he said, outside the house—"a very talented and agreeable girl. I never quite know whether she is chaffing, or whether she wants me to marry her. Poor thing! I suppose it's the latter—all girls do, somehow. Poor Popsy! More broken hearts."

Perhaps it is as well that we do not know always in what estimation we are held by our friends. Certainly, nothing was farther from

13—2

Miss Popsy's thoughts than to marry Dicky
Carew. I heard, indeed, last month that she
had gone to church with a highly respectable
young walking gentleman from the provincial
stage, and that they were both going out to Ca-
lifornia on a professional engagement. Marry
Dicky Carew, indeed! Popsy knew a great
deal better than that.

At the bottom of the stairs, on the ground
floor, he passed the hospitable door of Mrs.
Medlar; but he crept softly by on tiptoe.

"It is the shrine of material comfort," he murmured. "She is fat, she is fair, she is comfortable; she has still many summers of buxomness
before her; she has at least a hundred and fifty
pounds a year. When I sow my wild oats, I
will marry Mrs. Medlar, and let the others pine
away in cold neglect."

It was half-past eight, and he had a clear
half-hour before him. He spent it, and four-
pence, in a coffee-shop, where a cup of fragrant
mixture, whose component parts contained no
beans from sunny Mocha, with a slice of bread
and butter, formed his breakfast. He had but
little appetite for a breakfast, and sighed not

for luxuries. Contentment, after all, is a continual feast. At five minutes to nine he arrived at the gates of the British Museum. As the clock struck nine, he passed through them.

Nothing but the strongest sense of duty could induce me to reveal what followed in the next few minutes. This, however, is too imperative.

It may be known to some of my readers that there exists in the British Museum, for the use of readers only, a lavatory fitted with the customary jack towels, and supplied with soap. Mr. Carew sought this retreat with a calm, deliberate, and thoughtful air, as if he were about to remove the dust of a long walk, prior to study. Arrived there—he was happy in finding himself the first—he proceeded—oh, Dicky! Dicky!—to pick out and appropriate to himself the largest and best tablet of soap. The careful way in which he did this, the critical inspection of the soap, the honourable sense which led him to take but one, and leave the rest for his friends, all pointed to habit. This was too true. Among a certain body of advanced thinkers, moral philosophers whose code was based upon a broader view of right than most can boast, there had grown up, little by little, a custom of avoiding the small and annoying expense of buying soap by taking what was put out in the lavatory. They annexed for themselves what was meant for mankind. They substituted the particular for the general. By long habit they had grown inured to the custom, so that it had now none of the stings of conscious sin; and though they never spoke of it among themselves, they had come to regard the soap as a grateful but silent testimonial of regard from England to her men of genius. They may have been, and doubtless were, men of the keenest and most delicate sense of honour in other things; but there are, as everybody knows, secrets in every profession. Go to! We waste our breath in proclaiming the sins of other trades, but carry on our own. Let the publican put quassia in the beer, cocculus Indicus in the stout, fusel-oil and potato spirit in the sherry; let the grocer sand the sugar; let the parson play at being a priest; let Mr. Burls and his crew go on selling copies for originals; and let the obscure literary hack appropriate the soap in the lavatory, as he ap-

propriates his "copy" in the reading-room. It
is humble work that he does, and poorly paid.
Grub-street has been, it is true, long since
abolished, but its former tenants have only mi-
grated. When an Improvement Society de-
stroys a rookery, the rooks only go somewhere
else. Pope's poets and pamphleteers are dispersed at night ; but in the day you may find
them all in that vast circular apartment, where
light, pens, ink, blotting-paper, and warmth—
everything but air—are given, with the noblest
library in the world, without money and without price, to those who like to use them. Far
be it from me to defend Dicky's custom. I
only record it. The librarians lament the loss
of engravings from the books, which are cut
out and sold by the more needy among the
readers for one penny apiece. But the daily
loss of the soap has never yet, to my knowledge, formed the substance of a paragraph in
the annual report, a complaint posted up in
the room, or a parliamentary commission.

Mr. Carew wrapped his soap in paper, and
deposited it in his coat pocket. Then he re-
paired to the reading-room and began his work.

His labours—for he had postponed everything to the last day—were of a divided nature.
The mission of the *Weekly Intelligence* was to
show up the aristocracy in their true colours, to
paint the bloatedness of our prelates, and to
represent faithfully the down-troddenness of the
British workman. It was also devoted to the
purpose of hiding from the workman who
bought the paper the fact that he is in these
latter days falling into such a condition of mind
and body as no class of artizans have ever before experienced, inasmuch as he is incapable
of combining except for the purpose of getting
higher wages and lower hours, that he has
ceased to take an intelligent interest in his
work, that he lives for himself alone, and that
he drinks away all that he can spare from a
half-starved household. To conceal these home-
truths, and to reveal the other falsehoods, was
the *raison d'être* of the *Weekly Intelligence.*
Dicky, who was on the staff, was entrusted
with the easy work of showing up the vices of
the great.

On the other hand, the *Christian Clerk* was
a paper of an altogether different tendency.

Its object was to circulate among the Church congregations. It aimed at being the friend of churchwardens, and the companion of all Anglican vestrymen. It had no theological bias, but prostrated itself before everything that wore a white tie, and could use the letters M.A. For licentiate persons it had small respect. Dicky was an old and valued servant on the staff of this organ. He was regarded by the editor as an unfortunate and misunderstood man of genius. There was scholarship in his papers, lucidity and strength in his arguments, and a certain solid style, he would say, which one might look for in vain among other ecclesiastical papers.

Dicky began vigorously to look for material for the *Weekly Intelligence.* He took down half a dozen old volumes of the *Gentleman's Magazine*, all thumbed and worn by the exploring fingers of countless predecessors.

He had his paper ready at his right hand, and pen in hand to note anything that occurred. For some time the search was fruitless. His rapid eye ran up and down the columns without finding anything.

"I seem to know them all by heart," he

groaned. "It's disgusting to see how men find them out."

Then he took down another half-dozen, and began a new search. After a little he found something that seemed to suit his purpose, and began to write.

"In the yellow and faded pages of an old magazine"—Dicky always began his little anecdote paragraph this way—"we discover the following curious and interesting pieces of information."

And so on. By dint of going through a dozen volumes of Sylvanus Urban, he managed to pick out what amounted to nearly a column and a half of small type. There was a riddle, the wording of which he altered a little; there was a short account of a gentleman's seat, showing that it was one of the oldest mansions in England, to which Dicky added that its owners were the most profligate; there was a notice on the York Assizes, where no fewer than five and twenty were left for execution, two being respited—the indignant writer called attention to the fact that the judges were gentlemen; there was a report of an action in the West Indies, in which Dicky remarked that the common sailors, who did the fighting, got no mention. And so on, all being flat, stale, and unprofitable; for Dicky was long past the time when he used to try to put things pleasantly, and his *réchauffés* were served up week by week, without the slightest disguise.

The *Weekly Intelligence* finished, Mr. Carew turned his attention to the *Christian Clerk*.

This was a more important business. He was engaged upon a series of brief papers on the ecclesiastical questions of the day, and it behoved him to exercise considerable care to steer clear of theological difficulties. As Dicky's only principle in literature was to steal everything he wrote, and never to read without an eye to plagiarism, it was first of all necessary to discover safe ecclesiastical material. He found this among the pamphlets of the last century, a *corpus* of good work too often neglected by the starveling small fry of literature. If by any remarks of mine I can turn the petty plagiarist into a new, fruitful, and wholesome preserve, I shall be glad to indicate to him the road by which Dicky Carew might—alas, that I must write the word *might!*—have risen to literary distinction. Dicky was the original discoverer —he kept the discovery to himself—of the pamphlet. He loved it of all ages, but he loved it most for practical purposes a hundred years old; for then it was sure to possess some of the graces of modern writing. He would transfer anything he pleased simply by copying it out. Now, in earlier work there was often a passage, a turn of thought, or a phrase, too majestic in its roundness, or too involved, for the modern scribe. In such cases, Dicky had all the trouble of taking the idea and writing it over again himself. But the pamphlet kept for fifty or a hundred years in the wood, so to speak, acquired a fullness, a mellowness, and a delicacy of flavour quite unknown in the ephemeral productions of the day. He felt safe even with pamphlets thirty years old. They were quite sure to have been written by a man whose age would be somewhere about forty, so that the probability was very much in favour of his having gone to a world where plagiarisms are not sharply looked after—where, indeed, such things are impossible. Armed with one of these, Dicky boldly dipped his pen in the ink, and copied whole paragraphs, regardless of possible consequences.

On this day he wrote a careful and elaborate argument, from the Anglican point of view—*i.e.*, from a modern pamphlet dated about the year 1843—in favour of Church Establishments. The writer of the pamphlet from which he cribbed, one of the Oxford movement of that date, had not yet become convinced of the desirability of Church freedom with a view to reducing the laity to Church discipline, and therefore advocated Church and State. His successors have learned better. Nor had he yet, as those of the following generation have done, taught himself that overweening respect for authority which enables the Ritualist to see a friend and certain protector in Rome. Therefore he talked about the "errors" of the Roman Catholic Church. Dicky modernized his work to suit what he understood to be the latest phase of thought. At the close of his argument he allowed himself a few phrases of a really eloquent piety, with texts which he found at the end of the pamphlet. They were of the kind he liked—sonorous, well rounded, eminently Christian, and dogmatic. When Dicky folded up his papers in two parcels that evening, addressing one to the printer of the *Weekly Intelligence* and the other to the printer of the *Christian Clerk*, he felt that he had done a good day's work, and earned the humble stipend which he was receiving for labours of such great importance. The one envelope was full of blasphemy against all authority, divine or worldly; the other was, as hotel advertisers say, "replete" with the sweetest, the most sentimental, the most pious adhesion to all constituted authority, and especially to the Anglican bishops.

It was then five o'clock, and it must not be supposed that the day's work had been conducted entirely without refreshment. Not so. A select circle, comprising half a dozen of the choicer spirits, were wont to meet at one, and after the simple dinner of a chop or a sausage, with half a pint of stout, discuss the more abstruse literary topics over pipes and gin-and-water. Those who were in funds sometimes carried on these Tusculan disputations with such ardour, and so long, as to be too late to return to the Museum, in which case they would find their MSS. and the books from which they had last been stealing kept for them the next morning by their friends the attendants.

They were a seedy and generally a morose crew. Dicky alone among them preserved a cheerfulness which was mostly due to his splendid constitution. They were engaged in copying for scholars, in compiling for third-rate publishers, in inventing blood and thunder stories for the lowest periodicals, or, like Dicky himself, in writing for the papers which appeal to the class just removed from pauperdom. How they drifted into the calling of "letters" it is hard to say. Perhaps one or two of them had been gentlemen, and had been scholars. Possibly most of them had deserted the lower ranks of clerks, or begun, like Dicky, as ushers in commercial academies. Not one of them deserved better pay or higher consideration than he got; not one had a right to complain that he served a hard master, because all were such bad servants.

Among these friends Dicky drank a modest allowance—three glasses—and returned to his duties. It was the third glass which inspired

him with the happy thought of adding the
final clauses of pious ejaculation above referred
to. Perhaps it was the same glass which confused the keenness of his vision to a certain
extent, and made it possible for him to commit
the most fatal mistake of his life; for when he
addressed the manuscript, folded and neatly
tied up, by an inadvertence that he was destined
to regret all his life, he sent off the packet destined for the radical and even atheistic *Weekly
Intelligence* to the mild and religious *Christian
Clerk*, while that intended for the *Clerk* was
addressed to the *Intelligence.*

He then made the best of his way to the
offices of *Clerk* and *Intelligence*, which were in
two neighbouring streets, left his copy, marked
"immediate," for the printer, and then began to
think what he could do with himself till seven,
the earliest hour possible for the commencement of a "night." Dicky especially disliked
walking, because it wore out the heels of his
boots, and yet he generally found himself con-
demned to pace the stony-hearted streets alone
with his thoughts for nearly two hours every
day, the time between the closing of the Mu-

seum and the commencement of the symposium. To be alone with their thoughts is to some men a perennial source of happiness. To Dicky it was exactly the reverse. For solitude led him to look back at the past or forward to the future. Neither of these prospects afforded him the slightest pleasure.

CHAPTER IX.

WHEN Dr. Chacomb left Marion, she remembered the promise made to her pensioner, and hurried away from the Park. If you have a constant drag and drain upon your resources, you come, after a time, to regard it as a necessary evil, like a humpback or a stiff leg, and cease to think of it in the light in which it first presented itself, of an intolerable nuisance. Provided Mrs. Spenser confined her applications for help to herself, Marion hardly minded. It was but so much a week added to the burden she had to bear. The chief thing she feared was that some time or other this excitable lady would break her promise, and invade their lodgings, where Adie might see her.

Mrs. Spenser, desperately poor, as has been

shown, lived in about the most ignoble neighbourhood in all London, always excepting certain portions of Pentonville. It was in Sun-
court, St. Giles's, a place where every room held
a family, and many rooms held more than one
family each. She lived there with her son,
called, by reason of a St. Vitus's dance which
possessed the boy, and impelled him to kick
out at odd times, to the discomfiture and indignation of passers-by, Rickety Jem. She had
one room for herself and her son, and they
slept in opposite corners. Try, if you can, to
realize the degradation of a woman who had
indeed once been a lady, when she had one
room for herself and her boy of fourteen. The
infamies and miseries of poverty can all be
summed up in this. Nothing—not even insufficiency of food, insufficiency of clothes, or ab-
ject dependence—is so great an evil as the
enforced huddling together in one room of a
whole family. It is too horrible to tell of, too
horrible to think of.

Yet the people in Sun-court were not excep-
tionally vicious or wicked. There are courts
—one I know of, only a few yards north of

14—2

Mecklenburgh-square—where a decently dressed man who ventured to pass through in the day-time would be infallibly set upon and robbed, and where if a policeman dares to show his burly form he is saluted with flower-pots rained upon him from the windows, with other casual manifestations of an unpopularity that belongs to a class rather than to an individual. In Sun-court anybody might pass through at any hour with impunity. The policeman was looked on as not a friend exactly, but as a necessary evil. The inhabitants were harmless, except in one parti-cular, that they were poor. When people are poor, however, they are dangerous. It is a fact well known to modern legislators, just as it was known to Julius Cæsar, that a well-fed man is contented with the order of things. That is why, if a member of Parliament shows signs of making himself disagreeable, he is presented with something good in the shape of a com-missionership.

Mrs. Spenser lived partly on what she could extract from Marion, and partly on what she earned as a maker of cardboard boxes. Her son contributed his share by selling the *Echo*, cigar-lights, and such penny papers as he could beg from gentlemen at the Metropolitan railway stations. It was a miserable and precarious livelihood. She was a miserable and a discontented woman. She held herself aloof from her neighbours, on the plea that she was a lady. She tried, but ineffectually, to keep the boy separated from the other boys in the street, on the ground that his father was a gentleman. The people in the court called her Lady Spenser—a title which she accepted with a kind of gratitude.

How long does it take to reduce a lady to the lowest dregs? how long a gentleman to the level of the habitual criminal? It is a question one hardly dares to ask. We may pass from one stratum of life to another with greater ease than we like to think of. The descent of Avernus is steeper than we imagine. The difference between those who wear respectable clothes and those who do not is less than we are pleased to think. Thousands have found it easy to step across the gulf, and once across, all must perforce stay there. For the heaven of respectability is like Abraham's bosom, as described by Josephus — inasmuch as, if you once get out of it, you can never get back again.

It was not Marion's first visit to this dreadful den. She had been there once, a year before this. Then it was a bitter frost, and the depth of winter. She went to the place, resolved to tell the woman that she could do no more for her : it was when her resources had dwindled down to her fifty pounds a year. She thought it would be an injury to her own two helpless ones to do anything further for this wretched creature, who repaid her kindness with ingratitude, and threatened as often as she begged. But when she saw the miserable tenant of the room wrapped in a single blanket, without a fire, without a penny, trying to forget hunger in sleep, while her boy ran about the iron-bound streets crying his *Echoes* and his cigar-lights, her heart melted, and she refrained from saying what she meant to say. Since then, through fair weather or foul, whether she earned much money or little, the woman had her share of it. She was alternately defiant and humble. She threatened still, and begged. She was intemperate. She had not improved at all, and she was always a bitter grief and burden to Marion; but she could not be cast off.

It was a greater moral shock than the poor girl had ever known, to see this woman when they came to London—to know what she had been, and to see what she was. But the first visit to her lodging formed an epoch in her mind, because it revealed to her some of the dreadful things which lie unheeded at one's feet. For the first time in her life she found herself face to face with a hopeless misery which she could do next to nothing to alleviate, and that little at the expense of those who were also dependent upon her. And yet the woman had a claim too.

A lady—was it possible that she could ever have been a lady? What remains of ladyhood, what traces of the delicate blossoms which are nurtured by gentle breeding, could be discerned in this poor fallen creature? Surely none, save in her speech, which was soft and clear, and not yet disfigured by the toads, snakes, efts, and other dreadful things which fell from the mouths of her neighbours. That was all. The current

of her thoughts—like a river whose mouth gets
silted up, and so forms broad and malarious
lagoons—had lost all settled purpose, if it ever
had any, and was now dispersed in the marshy
flats of food-providing. If this was certain, she
began to think of the day's luxuries—now the
maximum of gin obtainable. She looked for
nothing more; she hoped for nothing more.
When she looked back, which was seldom, she
was tormented with Dante's worst sorrow, the
remembrance of former happiness. She had no
hope for the future, because she never looked
forward. As for the present, she knew now of
only three evils in the world—cold, hunger, and
pain: she acknowledged two delights—warmth,
and the imaginary paradise of intoxication. She
was a ruined and hopeless woman. But such as
she was—a miserable outcast, a creature lost to
virtue, an unrepentant Magdalene—she had a
claim upon Marion.

Marion found her working at her cardboxes.
There was no carpet, no blind or curtain, and
no furniture except a table and a chair. Mrs.
Spenser had the table covered with the mate-
rials, which she was cutting and shaping with

wonderful dexterity. Her features in repose
were haggard, but regular. She had once, assuredly, been beautiful. A mattress lay in the
corner, the sunlight upon it streaming through
the dirty panes of glass, and falling full on the
face of a boy who lay there upon his back. He
was a sharp-faced, bright-eyed boy, nearly fourteen years of age; but he looked very much
younger, because he was so small and thin.
He was dressed in the merest rags. By his
side lay a blanket. He was barefooted, his
cheeks were hollow and wasted, his skin had
the flush and brightness which belong to consumption, and he had a hacking cough.

"Is this your—your son?" said Marion, with
some hesitation.

"That is my son," Mrs. Spenser answered.
"Don't interrupt me; I've got some work come
in, and I am in an industrious mood. I've promised Jem some tea by and by. You can't sit
down, Marion Revel, because I've only got one
chair, which I want. Tell me what you think of
my boy. Tell me who he is like. Is he like
me, do you think? Look up, Jem, and show the
lady your face."

Jem turned his face obediently. Marion stooped, with a shudder, and patted his cheek. The boy was exactly like her sister Adie.

"Have you brought me some money, Marion Revel? If you have, put it on the table. You are a wonderful girl to come here at all. I wish I could get on without your help. I'm in a better temper than I was this morning. Don't be angry with me, will you? And don't think about what I say when I lose my head. I could not hurt *her*, you know."

She was changed since the morning, and spoke with a certain softness pleasant to hear.

"I can spare you ten shillings. Will that do?"

"It isn't much, but it must do."

"There's the rent, mother," said Jem, with a sharpness beyond his years. "Don't you forget the rent."

As he spoke, a St. Vitus's trembling of the limbs seized him, which explained at once why everybody called him Rickety Jem.

He half rose from the mattress, in evident pain.

"It is the cab that ran over him yesterday," said his mother. "Lie down again, my boy."

" I was going to get you the gin, mother."

Mrs. Spenser did not blush for shame; but she laughed, which was her only equivalent.

"Presently, my son. He knows his mother's ways," she explained. "I told you all about them long ago, Marion Revel. You can't say I ever hide anything from you."

"Alas, no!"

"Nor much from the boy. You shall hear. Jem, my beauty, who was your mother?"

"A lady she was; and much good that is to us."

He seemed to separate the mother who was a lady from the mother who was not.

"Much good indeed. It does not prevent her from making cardboxes for a living. Who was your father, Jem?"

"A gentleman he was. And much good that is to us."

Marion started.

"Don't be afraid, Marion Revel; the boy has nothing to do with you or yours. What else was he, Jem?"

"A villain; and mother was a fool to run away with him."

"What will you do to him when you meet him?"

"Kill him if I can," said the boy, viciously. "Rip him up, and cut him down, cos he's done all the mischief."

"There," said his mother; "some day or other I shall meet the boy's father—no matter when, because I can wait. Then my boy Jem will be tall and strong. He will remember the little catechism I taught him. You'll remember it always, Jem, won't you?"

She went on working her deft fingers, manipulating the card, and cutting the bright-coloured paper with swift activity while she talked.

"You'll remember when you meet him—he is a tall and handsome man—very tall and very handsome, careful about his hands, dresses expensively. He has got a face something like yours, Jem, when your face isn't like mine. You will be sure to know him. Get him in a secret place, and murder him. Tell him what it was for. Ask him if he remembers Carry—ask him if he tried to find out what became of his Carry; and then murder him. Marion Revel, this is good

training, isn't it?   It is all I am able to give
him.   His name, Jem, is Lillingworth.   He was
a captain once, in the army.   Now you know all
about it."

"Oh, it is too dreadful!" said Marion.   "Jem,
you know your mother is not in earnest."

"She is, though," said Jem, nodding his head
—"real good earnest.   She makes me say that
patter every day.   Lord! I know all about Captain Lillingworth.   He's my father, and I've got
to kill him."

"No, no; it's only make-believe, Jem.   Do
you not know it is wicked to talk about killing
any one?"

"Wicked!" said his mother—"as if he knows
anything about religion!   Do you think *I* could
teach him religion—I?"

"Have you never been to church, Jem?"

He shook his head.

"Not such a fool as that," he said; "one of
the boys was nabbed last Sunday for just looking inside.   Got locked up all night, he did, and
never done nothink."

"Have you never been to school, Jem?"

He shook his head again.

" One of the boys says we shall all have to go soon, and get whacked."

" Can you read ? "

" Yes, I can read some, but not much. I can read the bill for the *Echo*. See, I can write a little, too." He took a piece of chalk out of his pocket. " There "—he traced on the door the letters E C H O, only the C was turned backwards—" that spells ' Echo.' I've made it wrong somehow. Never mind, all the boys mostly can write 'cept me, and I'm learning myself."

" Does he know nothing at all, this poor boy? " asked Marion.

" Nothing," said his mother—" nothing. Best that he should know nothing. We have been thrown upon the streets together, he and I. Let him live in the streets all his life. We shall both die there."

" One of the boys knows a hymn," said Jem, after thinking the matter over.   " He learned it to me. I can say it all a'most :—

'Adama Neeve was made of clay,
    Such was his petty cree—'

I forget—yes, ' his petty cree.' " (Perhaps he meant pedigree.)

' And in the garden he could play
  If he'd obedient be.

' Adama Neeve he looked about;
  There were apples red and brown,
And he got a stick, and they turned him out
  'Cos he knocked the apples down.'

There's more, only I've forgotten it since the cab ran over me."

"Don't look at the boy that way, Marion Revel," cried his mother, stopping her work for a moment. "And what are you crying for? He's all right."

The boy proved upon the spot that he was all right by a violent fit of coughing, followed by a terrible shaking of his limbs, which seemed dislocated for the moment by the energy of St. Vitus.

"We've had a bad winter, and a long winter, too—that's given him a cough; and then came the cab. But we shall get on now, sha'n't we Jem, my pretty?"

Jem nodded and winked, trying to look jolly; then he shivered, and pulled the blanket round his neck. From time to time the fit seized him, when his limbs tossed themselves about without his control, and his teeth chattered.

"It is too dreadful!" Marion murmured.
"What can I do for you—what can I do?"

"It is not so dreadful as it looks. So long as
the weather is warm, I don't mind so much;
and Jem is a good boy, too—aint you, Jem?
When he's well he'll bring home sometimes a
couple of shillings a day, won't you, Jem?"

"Once I brought home three shillin's."

"So you did, Jem; so you did."

"That was when I held the gentleman's
horse, and he gave me half-a-crown and thought
it was a penny."

"I spent it all," Mrs. Spenser explained, de-
fiantly. "Jem had none of that windfall, poor
lad."

"One of the boys—" Jem began again.

"You *must* do something for the boy," Marion said. "Perhaps I shall be able—"

"Marion Revel, you let my boy alone, and I
will let your brother and sister alone—that is a
bargain. If I choose that the boy shall grow
up as he is growing up, that is my business; we
shall be revenged so, somehow, on his father. I
am a miserable woman, and he is a gutter boy.
Some day we shall find him out."

"Do not think of revenge. What good will revenge do?"

"You are a fool, Marion Revel?" the woman replied, in her clear silvery tones and her quiet manner. "Revenge is what I dream of. Every day that I wake in this den, and feel myself lower than I was yesterday, I think more and more of revenge. I want to make *him* suffer as he has made me suffer. I want to curse him through his son. He'll feel that, if he can feel anything, when he sees him."

Then Jem had another attack of coughing.

"One of the boys—" he began again, but choked.

"Let the man come here," Mrs. Spenser said. "Let him come here and look at the boy. Let him see us both; let him think what I am, and what I used to be before he came, with his handsome face; and then let us two, Jem and me, haunt him and follow him about wherever he goes—won't we, Jem?"

"All right," said Jem, whose notions of a vendetta were as yet imperfectly developed. "All right, mother. Rip him up and cut him down."

"Now go, Marion Revel. No; if you give me

any more money, I shall only spend it on myself. If you give me any furniture, I shall sell
that for drink when the fit comes upon me. I
have got enough money now, and Jem shall
have some tea to-night."

"And shrimps, mother. Let's have shrimps."

"Yes, and shrimps and bread and butter.
That's what Jem shall get. I shall have
gin."

She had preserved throughout the same defiant air. When she saw the tears in Marion's
eyes, she became more defiant still. When
the girl patted her boy's cheek, she had a
pang of jealousy; when she took her money,
she laughed with a little triumph. She was
never quite certain whether to regard Marion
as an enemy or a friend, but leaned to the
former.

"Let me come again to see Jem."

"You may see him any day you like; all you
have to do is to go down Holborn, where he
hawks the *Echo* and his cigar-lights. Ask any
boy there for Rickety Jem."

"I'm Rickety Jem," said the lad, with pride.

"Don't you see he is ill? Don't you notice

his cough and his bright eyes? And look how thin his cheek is," said Marion.

The mother tossed her work aside, and took the boy's head in her hands.

"Don't try to frighten me, Marion Revel. The boy's going to get strong and well. They are growing pains he has, and the winter's made him weak. Is not that so, Jem? Why, I feel him getting stronger every day."

"All right, mother," said Jem. "One of the boys said as another boy said as I wasn't going to be long for this world. Then we all laughed."

"Go away, Marion Revel. You will bring bad luck on my boy and me. You ought to, I'm sure. What can one of your name bring me, except misery?"

"Won't you let me come again to see the boy?"

"No—yes. Come if you like. What does it matter? After all, you are a good woman, Marion Revel." Her voice sank a little, but she raised it again. "It's a pity you're fallen off in your looks, because you were once a very pretty girl—a very pretty girl indeed. And now

15—2

your figure is quite gone, Marion." She had resumed her place at the table, and her fingers were nervously playing with her cardboard and scissors. "Sixteen years ago, now—you must have been eleven, and the others were seven and five. They were both like their mother, I remember, but you were like your father. A grave little girl you were, full of queer sayings. Oh, Marion, do you remember the questions you used to ask—such questions, which not even your father could answer?"

The tears came into her eyes as she recalled the old days, and her voice became unsteady. She waited a moment, and then went on, in a clear and deliberate tone—

"I used to lie awake at night and think of the other two, Marion; but I don't dare think of them any more—it drives me mad only to see either of them at your window. Not to see them at all, and to think of them still, would have driven me mad then; but I had my boy here to nurse, and that kept me in my senses. God knows it would have been better for me to have lost them quite. Sometimes I used to wonder what I did it for. Now I have long left

off wondering or thinking why I was so wicked
and so foolish. But once I used to think a good
deal about it. It was after he left me—left me
like a flower he had put in his button-hole one
day and thrown aside the next. He was a cruel
and a selfish man; he made me repent the very
day I did it. He never spared a woman in his
passion; he used to boast that to my very face,
when it was too late; he used to give me the
shameful history of all the women he had led
astray."

"Do not think of him," said Marion.

"Years ago, when Jem was a little baby, I
used to think of him every day and every night.
I used to curse him. One of my prayers was
heard—just think of that—because I learned
by accident that he disgraced himself, and was
obliged to leave the army. That was something,
but not enough. No, I want to see him lose all
the money that gets him the things that he
loves, and go down to the grave in miserable
poverty like this. He likes luxury of any kind:
let him make his dinner off a crust of bread, and
his supper off a red herring on lucky days.
Then I shall be satisfied. No," she added, "it is

not true. I shall never be satisfied, because I
never could forget what I lost. Oh, Marion!
Oh, the days gone by! Oh, the happy, peaceful
days when I was loved and trusted, and my
children put their arms round my neck and said
their prayers."

"God will forgive," whispered Marion.

"But will *he* forgive? No: it is impossible.
I haven't done any harm to God," she said,
wildly. "I could face Him. It is the *other*.
How could I ever bear to look at him
again?"

"He has long since forgiven every sin
against himself, because his own are forgiven.
Oh, believe it, and let your poor heart be
softened."

Marion bent her face and touched those guilty
cheeks with her own pure lips. The woman
shrank back with a little cry, and covered her
face again with her hands. It is hard to follow
the current of a mind like that of this poor
creature. For the first time, Marion seemed to
have roused in her some sense of human regret,
if not repentance. She was not, then, utterly
insensible. I believe that prison chaplains and

matrons tell the same story. There is no man
or woman so hardened but that there is some
weak point. Marion had found the weak point.
A little sympathy, a little patience, silence on
certain points connected with the past—these
things seemed to touch her.

But what hope, what future, was there possible, even if the better nature were thoroughly
awakened?

She sat silent at the table, and then she began
again with the pasteboard and the scissors; then
she spoke in a whisper, like the far-off murmur
of a shell—

"I don't think," she said, not looking up—"I
don't think there is a single woman in all the
world except you, Marion, who would do what
you are doing. Oh, how hard they are, all of
them, and unforgiving! Not but what it's right,
and what we ought to expect, Marion. You
must not bring yourself to any harm through
me. Would *they* like it if they were to find out?
Do you think you ought to come here? Remember everything. Make your heart hard
against me, my poor girl. I am only a drag
upon you. I take away your money as

fast as you get it; and you are afraid that
I shall say or do something to frighten the
other two. Do you think you *ought* to come
here?"

The soft, dreamy voice ceased. Then there
came a change in her face, swift and sudden;
but Marion could not see it, any more than she
could see the suspicions in her brain.

"Let me come again, for the boy's sake. It is
dreadful to see him so ill and so ignorant. Let
me come and teach him something."

Mrs. Spenser dashed the hair from her face,
and sprang to her feet, standing on the mattress
where her boy lay—large-eyed, wondering, ex-
pectant from long experience of a row—like a
tigress over her cub.

"No, no!" she cried. "Leave my boy alone.
You ought to hate him; you ought to wish him
dead; you ought to loathe his sight. Marion
Revel, why do you come here at all? What
right have you in this house? Go away, and
wait till I ask you for more money. I shall
work no longer. Why should I work for twelve
hours a day to earn two and twopence? Go
you, and make money to keep me and the boy,

as well as those other two helpless creatures. Go away, before I do you a mischief. Jem, you miserable son of a miserable mother, take this shilling and crawl out and get the gin. Now, Marion Revel, what do you say to that?"

CHAPTER X.

THE sunny nature, as we call it, is one so greatly lauded and envied that it goes to one's heart to criticize it. Nevertheless, the truth is that "sunniness" very often comes from sheer insensibility, and a dislike to disagreeable things. I fear that the sweet good temper always shown by Fred Revel, and his affectionate behaviour to his sisters, took their origin in these natural causes. He had small capacity for sympathy, a profound inability to calculate the chances of the future, and was impressed to so high a degree with a sense of the beauty of things beautiful, that it was, with him, almost a disease. Naturally, therefore, it cost him no effort to regard his sisters with affection, especially the younger, whose beauty he could see was a thing quite rare and unapproachable.

He thus made up in a measure for his laziness by his affection. He repaid devotion by gentle words, and even caresses. When he was at home —which was not often—he was at the orders of his sisters. He had been known to spare Marion a journey to Burls's shop; he would sometimes lie on the sofa and read to them; on Sunday he had occasionally gone to church with them; and on Sunday evenings, when Winifred Owen always came upstairs to have tea with his sisters, he stayed with them, helped in the preparation of the simple banquet, sang with Adie afterwards, and comported himself with all the steadiness of a Sunday-school teacher.

Unfortunately, these loving natures are like bindweed, convolvulus, or clematis, inasmuch as they are apt to spread the tendrils of affection in unexpected directions—other, in fact, than those of sisterly affection. It was not enough that the young man should be loved by his sisters—that is a kind of affection which does not satisfy; he craved for the deeper and fuller stream of passion. He found it with Winifred

Owen; and at this period of the history their love passages had already gone a very great deal farther than even Mr. Owen, jealous for his daughter, suspected. It is not, therefore, surprising to hear that, when Winifred's work at the telegraph office was finished, it often happened to her to find Fred Revel waiting to take her home.

The same thing happened to many of the young ladies in the department, and was indeed so common an occurrence as to excite no other feeling with those who went home unaccompanied than that of envy. None of these telegraph clerks, however, were waited for by persons of their own sex. It was also remarked that the gentleman who came for Winifred Owen possessed personal attractions of a higher order than most of the cavaliers in waiting. The girls of her Majesty's telegraph department are not, it must be understood, given to the dangerous practice of casual and meaningless flirtation. You will not meet them at theatres with gentlemen who hail from the Temple, nor are they to be accosted in Westbourne-grove by invincible young City men. Not at all: their behaviour is as circumspect as their position is respectable. There is no line of work in which a girl's reputation is safer than in the telegraph offices. Add to this, if you please, that her Majesty's Government—which is piling up pyramids of material for repentance in making contracts for work, which ought to be done at first hand, with people who get their profit out of the underpaid women in their employ—has not yet, happily, applied the dire and dreadful rule of supply and demand to the telegraph service. The girls are honestly paid and fairly worked, and they are not bullied like the poor girls in shops; so that they retain their self-respect.

Of course it was the one piece of folly wanting to fill Fred's cup that he should fall in love. Perhaps, if he had done it a year or two before this, when his indolence was not as confirmed as a bodily blemish, it might have been good for him. In a healthy state of education we shall train up the boys to fall in love as a duty at two or three and twenty. As it is, those of our youth who permit themselves this natural emotion at so early an age are the uncalculating and the sanguine, like Fred Revel.

How handsome he was, as he waited for the girl clerks to come out, and watched for Winifred among them! As yet, their wooing had the subtle charm of secrecy; and Fred belonged to the girl, though she alone knew it, by ties that could not be broken.

Her pulse beat higher with pride as she took his arm, and walked with him down the unfashionable street of Newgate. She loved him. It is assuredly not the first time that a woman has given her heart to a man whom she knows to be —soften it—deficient in the more robust virtues. The worthless ne'er-do-well has for her some secret charm of manner which the world fails to detect. Was not Mrs. Medlar in love with Dicky Carew? Was not Bluebeard idolized by every one of his wives in turn? Did not Acte, the sweet and pure-minded Christian, love Nero, the Anti-Christ? As if we wanted examples! Winifred loved this handsome and indolent young Absalom, who, for his part, loved the bright-eyed little telegraph girl as much as it was in his nature to love anybody.

"We must be more careful, Winifred," said Fred, in his airy manner. "You know what they say—I mean in the lower classes, of course —about keeping company? What an expression! They will think in Lowland-street that we are keeping company, will they not?"

Winifred had heard the expression employed in her own department.

"They have not the chance," said Winifred, squeezing his arm; "we are too clever for them, because we always part at the corner of Tottenham-court-road."

"Not to-night, my love," he replied. "I have got some money; let us have a drive in a hansom through the parks."

"Fred, dear," she said, timidly, "I should like it so much—oh! so much! but would it be quite right? Do you think we ought? You know yesterday poor Adie had no dinner, because there was no money."

He was silent for a moment, and something like a blush crossed his face.

"I did not know," he said. "We will walk."

They walked, and he talked.

"I wish your father liked me, Winifred. It is a bore, considering everything. I met him on the stairs this morning, and he stopped to say, with a long face, 'Young man, the soul of the sluggard desireth, but hath nothing. Have you found any work yet?' Any work, you know; as if I was a common clerk or a railway porter."

"Well, but, Fred"—Winifred was jealous for her father—"what else should he say? You do want work, do you not?"

"Say? Anything. But then, Winifred, you do not understand—how should you?" He laid his hand upon hers. "What a pretty little hand it is! I think I shall never get tired of it—and mine, isn't it?"

"All yours, Fred, dear."

"Let me buy it a new pair of gloves."

To be sure, Winifred's gloves were a good deal worn, and showed signs of frequent repair. I do sincerely believe that her character will be greatly raised when I state that she had the courage to refuse a new pair, on the same ground as she had refused the drive—the plea of poverty.

"Then, Winifred, if I must not give you anything, let us go somewhere where we can have a quiet talk together."

It was, as has been stated a chapter or two back, in the sweet spring month of April, when the sign of the zodiac—whatever the zodiac may be—is Gemini, the twins, as we call them, but the older astronomers named the Maid and the Man —that is to say, it was the acknowledged season of love. Over in the west—for it was seven o'clock—the sun was going down behind a lurid mass of sapphire, smoke, and blood-red cloud. Fred hurried his companion away from the tumult of Holborn into the quiet retreat of Lincoln's Inn-fields. He opened the gate of the gardens with a key, to which he certainly had no right, and took Winifred into the quiet gardens, where the lilac was bursting into bloom, the trim lawns were fragrant from an afternoon shower, and the tulips were gorgeous in their short-lived splendour: a Cockney garden, if you please, but pleasant and sweet to the girl.

"Let us walk up and down here," said her companion. "It is always quiet and undisturbed, and we can talk."

The gardens were quite deserted—there was no one to listen to them, no one to see them, no one to disturb them. An ideal place for a London idyll. Winifred's lover walked beside her, as beautiful as Apollo; his head thrown back with a careless grace that you may see in the early portraits of Byron, his eyes flashing, his lips, like Adie's—half parted, the very type and ideal, to outward seeming, of early manhood, full of noble thoughts and lofty aims. He looked strong and resolute, because he was dreaming great things as he walked. He was on a Royal Road to greatness—such greatness as means wealth and comfort; and was marching along it in imaginary state and splendour, with Winifred beside him.

She did not share his dreams, this simple girl who was in love with him, but she looked up·at him with eyes that drank in long draughts of admiration. Heavens! that such a hero—so brave, so handsome, *going to be so good*—should see anything in her, the telegraph girl, to love; and what—what must be the nobleness of the man who could so stoop beneath him as to marry her? Yes, to marry her. Winifred was married; Fred Revel was married; they were actually married to each other. They went to the parish church one Sunday morning—Mr. Owen never went to any church at all, but stayed at home, to read either Plutarch or the Book of Proverbs

—where the banns had been put up among half a hundred others, and were married; and no one, not a soul, knew anything about it. It was just before her father's warning, which, like many a prophetic announcement, came too late to be of any use; and the words never ceased to ring in her brain.

" He's a worthless chap, my girl."

"Winifred," Fred began, bending his gracious head with such a sweet condescension as the king who reigned in Shushan from India to Ethiopia might have observed to that fair Jewess Esther after her twelvemonth's washing in oil of myrrh and sweet perfumes, or as Solomon bestowed upon the nameless nymph whose lips were as a thread of scarlet—" Winifred, my dar-ling, do you think, like all the rest, that because I have done nothing yet, I *can* do nothing?"

The girl shook her head at these assuring words. Of course she did not.

" And suppose—suppose, Winifred—that I were to come to you with such a position as would be worthy of you—"

" Fred, I am only a telegraph girl, but, oh, so proud of you!"

16—2

"The wife takes her husband's position," he replied, with the grandest air. Had he been the Earl of Burleigh, his condescension could not have been greater. "As my wife you will be, not Mrs. Revel, but Madame la Comtesse. Would you like that? For I intend to resume the title which my father dropped as soon as we get back into our old position."

"But—but—oh, I am not fit to be a great lady."

"You will learn, Winifred—you will easily learn. Marion and Adie will teach you. You are quick and clever. I shall not be ashamed of my wife."

"To be your wife before all the world!" she gasped. "It takes away my breath."

"Sit down," he said, "and let us talk about it calmly."

He placed her on a garden seat, and sat by her, taking her hands in his. It was as yet all too much happiness for the girl, who with him could only breathe and feel.

"They call me idle, I know," he said, thinking over Dr. Chacomb's accusing speech. "They think I am good for nothing but loafing about and playing billiards. It is not true, Winifred. Adie will tell you, if you ask her, that I am always thinking about what I shall do. Why, I am ready to do anything—anything that a gentleman may do, and never afterwards be ashamed of. They shall see—they shall see what I will do."

Winifred was wholly carried away by the infection of his ideas.

" Adie is right," she cried. " She always says you have the noblest of hearts."

"Adie is the best girl in all the world. Now, Winifred, dear, I am going to tell you a great secret."

" What is it, Fred ?"

" Do not laugh, and do not tell any one. When I was in France with Lord Rodney Benbow, I was told by a woman from Algiers, an Arab woman, that there were to be great troubles before me, but that after three or four years all would be smooth. Then my father died suddenly — killed by a fall, and then all our troubles began. As for Adie and myself, we have always felt that we should pull round somehow."

"But do you believe what a fortune-teller says?"

Winifred had been brought up in a healthy contempt for the petty supernatural.

"No—that is, I believe we shall get out of the hole we are in somehow. Of course, I do not believe what a fortune-teller says"—but he did—"and I have plenty of irons in the fire. I will tell you: first, I have put down my name at the Colonial Office; then I have applied for a nomination to the Foreign Office. If these do not come to anything I have promised a man I know—not a gentleman—a bonus of ten per cent. on any good thing he gets me. Unfortunately, all the secretaryships are given to men who can put capital in the company. Besides this, Dicky Carew thinks he knows a paper where they would like a man to send West-end things to them."   Fred spoke as if he belonged without a doubt to the highest stratum. "Out of all this something will come, surely.   What would you like best? They might make me governor of some small West Indian island to begin with. Should you like that? 'His Excellency Sir Frederick Revel,

K.C.B., Governor of the Starboard Islands, accompanied by Lady Revel, has returned to England on furlough, and yesterday dined with the Queen at Osborne.' That would read well, wouldn't it ? Or they might make me secretary of legation at Vienna. Society is not so good at Vienna as it used to be, I fear, but we need not be too particular; and it is a place where we could make ourselves comfortable. Or perhaps you would prefer being attached to the embassy at Paris? There may be a better chance for a diplomatist, especially one of French descent, in Paris."

"Oh, Fred!"—the prospect was altogether too dazzling, and she gasped, "I can never become a great lady—never! I shall only make people laugh at you, for marrying such a simple girl. How will you like to have ladies laughing at my want of manner?"

"I have thought of all that," he replied, as if the thing were quite settled, and nothing left but to arrange the details—"I have thought of all that. Before we leave town, you shall live for a few weeks with a family who will form you. Your taste in dress is already perfect—

almost as perfect as Adie's; and yours is a style of beauty which can bear ornament, which hers can do without. I think you would look very well with a diamond spray in your hair. I saw one the other day in Bond-street which I thought would just do for my pretty little girl. I mean some day to deck you up in all the dainty things that money will buy. Then, if you like, you shall learn some accomplishments—playing, singing, languages — all the little trifles that women pick up so easily." He spoke as if they came by nature, or were to be learned in a week or two. "The chief business is, of course, the cultivation of manner and style. You must be, above all things, *chic*. We should have to sink the school and the connection with the—eh?— the Government department."

"Fred, I could never learn to be ashamed of my father."

"Ashamed? no, I suppose not. Only it will not do when we are in society to put the fact of the school in the foreground. A countess, you know, may be the daughter of anybody, but she does not generally tell all the world about it."

Winifred was silent. This kind of talk jarred upon her.

"And now that we are united, Winifred," the Prince went on, in a lordly way—"now that I have married you and made you happy, you will take pains to fit yourself for the position you will occupy, will you not?"

"Yes, Fred," she answered him, humbly. "I will try all I can; only you must tell me what to do. Perhaps Adie will help me."

"But remember, dear, it must be a profound secret. I do not want anybody, not even Adie, to know anything about it. I can meet you in the evening, when you leave the office, and we can walk home together and talk; but no one need know till we are able to tell them—till I am able to take you away altogether."

"Oh, let me tell my father, Fred—poor father! And he loves me so!"

"Certainly not—on no account. I would rather you told Adie even. Only wait a little while, dear child, and we will tell all the world. Wait just a little. They must give me something good, with all my interest." At the moment he pictured to himself the whole of the Upper House tumultuously pressing his claims on dispensers of official sinecures. "Why, a commissionership in the Poor Law is worth about a thousand a year, and nothing to do for it. I should not be at all surprised if Rodney got me that."

"Are you quite sure, Fred?" (Winifred remembered what her father had told her. She blushed to remember that it came through a waiter)— "Are you quite sure that Lord Rodney is your friend?"

"Sure, Winifred? Why, we were friends at Oxford, and we got rusticated for the same thing. Then we were to have gone to Egypt together, only I did not get so far. Friends! why, Rodney would do anything for me—anything in the world."

It was an *idée fixe* with the young man that his one acquaintance in the world who had position had also unbounded influence, and was exercising it for him day and night.

As a matter of fact, Mr. Owen's information was perfectly correct. Lord Rodney, who had as yet no influence whatever, was tired of constantly lending money to a man who seemed in-

capable of doing anything for himself. He resolved—and his resolution was arrived at, un-
luckily, just before this very evening—to give
Fred Revel no more money.

"Come, Winifred," he said, "there is no one
here; put your arms on my neck, so. Now kiss
me, and say you love me."

She did as she was told.

"And I have made you happy?"

"Yes, very happy. Oh, Fred, Fred!" she
burst out crying—"you *will* leave off going to
billiard tables, and—and—work, and be good to
your sisters, will you not?"

He was moved by her tears, but very angry
at her words. Work! Leave off billiards! Trifles of this kind, when he was glowing with the
prospect of future greatness!

"That shows the kind of thing people say
of me," he replied. "Well, there is nothing to
be done but to leave the beastly hole where we
are now, and go somewhere else. I shall see
Rodney to-morrow, and tell him that he must
get to work in earnest for me."

"Forgive me, Fred."

"I forgive *you*, my dear," he said, magnanimously; "but I do not forgive people who try to set you against me. There, let us have no more tears. Come, my dear, you are married to me now, and you must believe in me, you know."

" Yes, Fred."

Winifred was very humble as they left the garden. She clung to her lover's arm, because her eyes were full of tears, and her brain was turning round and round. He was silent too, because, as will happen in every fool's paradise, a word of the girl had knocked over his palace walls about his ears. It was as if the sun was suddenly hidden behind the clouds.

Was Lord Rodney his friend?

If not, then he had nothing to hope from any one.

Would he give up billiards, and work and be good to his sisters?

Two of the four sovereigns he had taken from Adrienne were in his pocket still. Where were the other two? And what about the debt—the debt of which his sisters knew nothing?

They parted sadly at Tottenham-court-road, with a silent shake of the hand. The young man walked along Oxford-street, moody and miserable. Presently he came to a door at which his feet stopped of their own accord, and without any volition on his part. Then they turned to the right, went up certain steps, and entered a room where three or four men were playing billiards.

The marker nodded familiarly. As Fred took down his cue, he whispered to him—

"The bill falls due in a day or two."

"Renew it, then, as you did for me last time."

"Can't, Mr. Revel—can't. The other party wants his money."

Fred made no answer. He replaced the cue, and presently left the billiard-room, to wander backwards and forwards in the street.

Work? He *could* not work.

Winifred went home. Her father was out, and she sat down, trying to think over what had happened. She was as sad as her lover. Was this right? Was this the way in which young ladies should be wooed, won, and married? Why, he had made sure, to begin with, that she loved him. So she did; but it seemed strange that he should assume it from the very first. And he had ordered matters his own way, without a word of remonstrance from her. She had begun the wifely obedience while yet a maid.

"He is a worthless chap."

Her husband! Husband of a fortnight—married in St. Andrew's, Holborn.

Her father's words rang in her brain with a dreadful pertinacity. She knew that they were true. In her heart she knew that all these fine promises would end in nothing. She foresaw the unhappiness she might be bringing upon herself. And yet, like Marion, towards whom Fred might sin seventy times seven and still be forgiven, she loved him none the less. For it was the strange property in the boy's character that all women who knew him loved him, and all men who knew him liked him; and yet all, somehow, despised him.

She loved him; that was all. She went to her bed-room at the back, and prayed for him. She gave him what she had—her prayers and her love.

When her father came home at nine o'clock,

he found Winifred bright and cheerful. The simple family supper was on the table, and the lamp was lit.

Winifred was rather silent.

At ten she put her work together. It was her wont to leave her father to smoke his pipe by himself.

"Father," she whispered, kissing the rugged and wrinkled face, which looked always so beautiful and kind to her—"father, if Fred Revel turns out different to what you thought, you will take back your words, won't you?"

"What words, my dear?"

"You said he was worthless. You meant that he could do no work, you know."

"Winifred!" he started up in his chair, took both her hands, and looked at her. She tried to lift her eyes, but could not.

"No, father, no," she sobbed; "ask me no questions."

He drew her to his knees, and held her as he had held her many thousands of times, when she was a little thing, and he was father and mother both to her. His left arm was round her waist, and her head was on his shoulder, and he was soothing and patting her cheek.

"My child, my daughter, my own Winifred!" he said, "tell me what you like—what you like, my dear. Forget what I said. No doubt I am a fool, and he is full of good qualities—as good as he is handsome; and nobody could be handsomer than he is. Only remember, my dear, what I have taught you. A virtuous woman—her price is above rubies. Be good, my child. Promise me—no, promise me nothing; only be good, my child."

She left him presently, but the schoolmaster had no sleep that night. His passionate Welsh nature was on fire with indignation against the handsome boy who had stolen away his child's heart. He walked up and down the room; he lay down, but could find no rest.

"If he does her any harm," he said; "if he plays his game of gentleman with my girl—I—"

In the morning, he was quite grave and silent during breakfast, making no observations at all out of Solomon's Proverbs. Winifred gave him his tea, with downcast eyes. When she rose to go to her work, she said, hesitatingly— .

"Father, you do not think the worse of any man because he is poor, do you?"

He shook his head and brightened up, seeing his opportunity.

"A good name," he replied, "is rather to be chosen than great riches; and loving favour rather than silver and gold. Winifred, find me, if you can, a single question that Solomon does not answer. Go to your office, my dear, and don't fret. 'A merry heart doeth good like a medicine.'" When she had gone, his face clouded again. "I wish," he said, "that the passages about fools and folly were not so fresh in my mind to-day. Solomon had a wonderful eye for a fool—'The father of a fool hath no joy.' To be sure, I shall only be his father-in-law."

Then the clock struck nine, and he went into the school and caned Candy Secundus. Invigorated by his anxiety, he inflicted upon that culprit a most astonishing punishment; insomuch that when he went home, his mother drew the inference of greater criminality than was absolutely the case, and gave the unfortunate boy a second caning before he went to bed, to

enforce and underline the lesson.   To Candy
Secundus, therefore—it is a remarkable instance
how men and women live unconsciously for each
other—Fred's wedding brought two chapters of
Lamentations, forming both a morning and an
evening lesson.

CHAPTER XI.

I T is not an easy thing for a physician to get away from patients, even at the beginning of the London season. But it was absolutely necessary for Dr. Chacomb to see his unfortunate cousin after this new misfortune which had befallen him. For his own part, he took the blow with the serenity of one who had received many buffets from fortune. If there should be a child, farewell to his heirship. If the woman played her cards well, farewell to his rule at Chacomb. In any case, it was a serious check on his projects; for he meditated great improvements on the estate. Taking the position of a country gentleman, just as the heir presumptive to an earldom might almost consider himself a peer, he gave his attention to questions affecting land, contracts with tenants, drainage, high farming, and other things. He talked over these subjects with authority, as one personally interested, and, in fact, enjoyed the additional importance accruing to him as the future possessor of a goodly heritage.

No light owned by Dr. Joseph Chacomb was at this period allowed to burn under a bushel, or, indeed, to burn at all save at such times as might be beneficial to himself. He owed, in fact, everything to the Chacomb estate. An adventurer, a shady general practitioner, a projector of companies which, if they were floated, always came to wreck, a haunter of tenth-rate clubs, where very questionable gentlemen associated to drink and tell stories, he found suddenly, ready to his hand, the rents of his cousin's property. He borrowed—who could resist the temptation of borrowing? He founded with great pains his Royal Hospital for Gout, on which he mounted the ladder of professional reputation. He left his old companions—the bond of friendship among the impecunious is like that among savages, uncertain and liable to sudden tempests of suspicion. He put off the habits and language of their class; changed his channel of thought; cultivated those manners which make the man; and became—a gentleman.

It required careful observation and long familiarity now to distinguish any trace of his twenty years' vagabondage in the polished doctor. He even became an author, and published that treatise of his "On Gout and its Cognate Diseases" which is still the standard work on the subject, although Dr. Porteous, of Savile-row, always declared that it was translated from the French—a language which Joseph Chacomb had learned in its purity in the Quartier Latin. He had a solid-looking house in Adelaide-street, Carnarvon-square; he had a professional carriage, with the Chacomb arms, and the soberest of liveries; he had a large medical and general library; he had a servant—the prince of servants—a man whose manners proclaimed him born to be a master of a college; he had a circle of acquaintance, creditable in themselves, and likely to advance his reputation; he gave dinner parties, at which he told admirable stories. All these things were done and established. Chauncey

Chacomb might develop into a Brigham Young in the matter of wives without affecting the doctor's position, credit, and prosperity. All this was his by right—subject, of course, to the few thousands he had borrowed. He was unmistakably chief physician of the hospital, he had undoubtedly composed a great work, and his doors were besieged by clients.

If there was an air of mystery about the doctor's antecedents, that helped him. Joe Chacomb the adventurer was gone and forgotten. In the new doctor, who sprang suddenly into reputation, people saw a man who was reputed to belong to an excellent Devonshire family, to be the heir of a large property, and who had spent the greater part of his life abroad in the pursuit of science—one who had travelled much, and observed a great deal. Dr. Porteous went so far, indeed, as to hint that perhaps he had travelled in the Isle of Portland, but that did no harm.

His prospects and professional name could not be hurt by Chauncey's conduct. What the doctor felt was a mixture of chagrin that he had been outwitted, pity for his cousin, and anger with himself for not looking after things more closely.

. Outwitted by his own creature—the woman he had sent down because he could trust her; a woman whom he had known for twenty years, and whom he had employed as the first matron of the new hospital until he thought she would be more useful as housekeeper to Chauncey!

"It will be worse for her in the end," he said. "I know her. She will find it grand at first to order the people about; then she will feel dull because no one will call upon her; then her temper will break out—Julia always had the devil's own temper; and then—poor Chauncey! It's a deuced annoying business."

Chauncey, too, whose muddled brain was growing every day feebler and less able to bear excitement; who followed him about like some tame pet when he went to Chacomb; who was only to be trusted because he was harmless— what would be the effect of a nagging and discontented woman upon him? His health was daily failing—he wanted the gentlest treatment; and here was a headstrong and self-willed wife, in whose clutches he would be as a little child.

Joseph Chacomb was a kind-hearted man, albeit there were certain specks and blemishes, already indicated, on his character. He felt that Chauncey, now that he was clearly cracked, and that Gerald was lying dead in some African swamp, was specially under his own care. Chauncey belonged to him, and he would not brook any interference in his conduct of this interesting case.

Who could help feeling pity for a man so shipwrecked and afflicted? particularly when his hallucinations were accompanied by a sincere trust and faith in himself, the doctor.

It was a disarrangement of his comfortable plans. Chauncey would not last long. Far from him the desire to wish his end—that would be unworthy of a man in his position; but soberly, in the nature of things, he could not disguise from himself, he said, the fact that Chauncey could not last long.

And then?

Chacomb Hall, with Marion.

The doctor was lonely in his grandeur; his

evenings were dull and stupid. Sometimes he
even longed for the jolly old days when he
would take his pipe to a club where certain
jovial fellows might be found, and where present
insufficiency of means—an admitted fact not to
be disguised—did not prevent the flow of cheerfulness. He was not a reading man, and he
had gradually got into the habit of imagining
Marion sitting opposite to him, playing to him,
presiding over his house, acting hostess to his
guests.

"She is a lady, by gad!" he would say.
"Dress her up, put a little more fulness in her
cheeks, give her eyes a look less anxious, take
that droop out of her mouth, and she'd be a
credit to an earl. She's worth fifty of her sister.
With those two in this house, with Chacomb
Hall to fall back upon, what society is there in
London that would not be open to me? I should
get known to—to Cabinet Ministers, perhaps. I
would get a title—Sir Joseph Chacomb, Baro-
net, M.D., of Chacomb. It is quite time that a
Chacomb should distinguish himself. Dr. Porteous would go into an apoplexy. Perhaps there
would be a little—eh? a little Joseph, successor

and heir. I should like to have a son; I should like to bring him up as I ought to have been brought up myself. What a splendid boy the son of Joseph Chacomb, properly brought up, would be!"

It will be seen that the doctor was human in having this weak side to his character. He could be sentimental; he liked to dream—being, as a rule, the most practical of creatures—of a future consisting wholly of domestic bliss.

"The old lot would laugh," he said to himself, "if they heard me. What fools men are! When one fellow blusters against religion, and society, sham morality, and the rest of it, the other fellows imitate, if not believe him: they bolster up their miserable make-believe of social revolt by the example of the man they think the strongest. Lord, Lord! Joe Chacomb was the advanced thinker; he was the materialist; he was the man who believed nothing and feared nothing. Look at him now; and where are all the rest? Gone back to the hearth—*Christiani ad focos*—sitting as meek as mice with their wives and children; going to church every Sunday; churchwardens; attendants at lectures; moral and religious parents, acquiescing in the order of things as they are; forgetful of the old discussions. Do they really forget, though? Is Paris as if it never existed? They used to admire Joe Chacomb, who was afraid of nothing. By gad! they shall admire me more now, and with better reason."

END OF VOL. II.

www.ingramcontent.com/pod-product-compliance
Lightning Source LLC
Chambersburg PA
CBHW020348030726
47496CB00007B/2045